T0129012

THE
ABDUCTIONS

THE
ABDUCTIONS

BOOK TWO OF THE MATTHEW
MORETTI AND HAN LI SERIES

ALAN REFKIN

iUniverse®

THE ABDUCTIONS
BOOK TWO OF THE MATTHEW MORETTI AND HAN LI SERIES

iUniverse books may be ordered through booksellers or by contacting:

iUniverse
1663 Liberty Drive
Bloomington, IN 47403
www.iuniverse.com
1-800-Authors (1-800-288-4677)

ISBN: 978-1-5320-4762-6 (sc)
ISBN: 978-1-5320-4764-0 (hc)
ISBN: 978-1-5320-4763-3 (e)

Library of Congress Control Number: 2018904532

Print information available on the last page.

iUniverse rev. date: 05/30/2018

PREVIOUS BOOKS BY ALAN REFKIN

Fiction

The Archivist, by Alan Refkin

Nonfiction

The Wild Wild East: Lessons for Success in Business in Contemporary Capitalist China, by Alan Refkin and Daniel Borgia
Doing the China Tango: How to Dance Around Common Pitfalls in Chinese Business Relationships, by Alan Refkin and Scott Cray
Conducting Business in the Land of the Dragon: What Every Businessperson Needs to Know About China, by Alan Refkin and Scott Cray
Piercing the Great Wall of Corporate China: How to Perform Forensic Due Diligence on Chinese Companies, by Alan Refkin and David Dodge

To my wife, Kerry
To Stanley and Betty Fitch

CHAPTER

1

The construction project had taken three years, not because it was especially complicated but because it was a secret. In the end, only one man would know what had been built, and that knowledge would be passed on to his successor alone—and to each subsequent successor in the same manner—in a perpetual chain of knowledge.

The two hundred workers toiled night after night in the stifling humidity and bone-chilling cold of the changing seasons, working only after dark so that no one could witness their presence. None of those who labored through the backbreaking work were allowed to return to their villages when their daily tasks were complete. Instead, before dawn, they were taken out a secret exit and escorted to a nearby compound. There they were fed well and given drink, and on occasion women were brought in for their pleasure. The workers considered themselves fortunate that they didn't have to claw out a daily existence like so many others throughout their country. Each was recruited because of his particular skill, and each was made to understand that he could not return to his home for several years if he accepted the work that was being offered. Their mysterious employer promised, through the person recruiting them, that their families would receive their wages during this time and would be well cared for.

ALAN REFKIN

As proof of the employer's sincerity, those who accepted the offer of work were given a pouch of gold as a bonus.

The payments and work continued for three years. Then the information that the project was complete worked its way up the supervisory chain of command, ultimately reaching the employer. The following day, the workers were told to stay in their compound because a party was to be held in their honor before they returned home. In the early afternoon, a great amount of drink and food was brought in, and everyone feasted until they could consume no more.

While his workers were celebrating, the employer inspected their work, just as he'd done daily for just over three years. He expressed his satisfaction that everything had been done correctly and that the completed project would protect him and his family in times of peril. He then instructed his assistant to make very generous payments to the families of those who had labored in this effort.

Later he ordered that everyone involved—the workers, the soldiers guarding them, the staff who had overseen the project, and even the assistant to whom he was speaking—be given poison with their meal. The face of the person receiving this command slowly changed from shocked disbelief to acceptance because the power of the person speaking with him was absolute. A secret was a secret only if no one knew about it, the employer went on to say.

Later that day, when the employer opened the wooden shutters in his quarters, he saw billowing smoke in the distance. He knew it was coming from the walled enclosure that housed the workers; he owned the entire hill on which their housing was situated, and there were no other structures in that area. When he could no longer see any smoke, he ordered a small group of his most trusted advisers to bury the bodies and erase any evidence of the workers' existence. He demanded silence from those who performed this task. No threat was needed, however, for all knew that anyone who broke that pledge would suffer the same fate as the dead men.

In time, the dense hillside bushes encroached on the fire-scarred compound and hid what had occurred there. Those who carried out the command to bury the bodies had not been told what those victims had done to deserve the punishment they received. But that was wholly unimportant. The emperor of China was the Son of Heaven, and his commands were considered sacred edicts to be followed even at the cost of one's life.

Kundek Temuujin was thirty-two years old, six feet five, and three hundred pounds of hard muscle. Born in Baotou, Inner Mongolia, a city at the edge of the Gobi Desert, he began working in a steel mill at the age of fourteen. Eight years ago, he caught the attention of Wang Lei, a Chinese industrialist who had been touring the factory. Impressed with his size and physique, the defense contractor had offered him a job as a bodyguard.

The giant Mongolian had no facial hair and a moon-shaped face that was twice the size of a normal person's. He shaved his head so close to the scalp that he was effectively bald. His permanent scowl told the story of someone who'd experienced none of the joys of life, only its tragedies, and anyone who looked at him instinctively cowered.

Kundek did not feel any regret for what he was about to do. He was a murderer, and that's exactly why he was here—to kill someone. He grabbed the woman lying on the floor and positioned her exactly where she should be, then placed the man next to her. Both he'd rendered unconscious with a single blow to the side of the head before binding their hands and feet with soft cloths and placing gags in their mouths. As he removed the .22 handgun from his pocket and pointed it at the helpless woman, she opened her eyes. He saw the horrified look on her face, which would soon be frozen and add to the credibility of the scene. Perfect. He pulled the trigger, and the woman's head slammed back against the hardwood floor with a dull thud.

Having regained consciousness after hearing the gunshot,

the Mongolian's next victim was frantically trying to wiggle away, but Kundek grabbed him by his shirt collar and dragged him back. He held the man with one hand while, with the other, he wiped the .22 handgun with a handkerchief to remove his prints. Then he put the weapon in the palm of the man's hand, forced the man's finger onto the trigger, and then wrapped his own enormous hand around both. The man bucked and gyrated wildly, trying to get away, but the Mongolian outweighed him by a buck and a half. He placed a tree-trunk-sized knee onto his victim's chest to hold him down. Moving the gun to the man's head, he positioned it exactly where it needed to be and forced the man to pull the trigger. Blood and brains blew out the back of the skull, and he released his grip and let the gun fall to the floor. He quickly untied and ungagged both bodies, then left through the back door before anyone came to investigate the gunshots.

Bone tired, David McAlister ran his hand over his bald head and down his day-old stubble. It was two in the morning. He knew he'd have more stamina if he lost forty-five pounds off his five-foot-eight frame, but the habits that had gotten him there over the past year were unlikely to change. When his now ex-wife had taken everything in the divorce and the judge had ordered a huge chunk of David's paycheck to be paid for alimony and child support, there had been nothing to look forward to except drinking and eating.

Everyone else had long since left the office, and with any luck, he'd be going home shortly. He'd spent the past eight hours documenting in intricate detail what he believed would prove to be the discovery of the century. Now all he needed to do was email the home office in London, inform them of what he had uncovered, and include images for the corporate naysayers who would otherwise try to stab him in the back.

Earlier David had thought about telling his fellow engineers before they left for the day, but he had decided against it. They'd want to jump on the bandwagon and take any credit they could for his hard work, his intuition—and, yes, his good luck. But they'd just have to find another way to climb the corporate ladder. He wasn't sharing this with anyone. He felt a momentary twinge of guilt that his Mongolian assistant, Zaya Batbayar, wouldn't get credit, even though Zaya had found the entrance. That fact, of course, would be missing from his report. If anyone learned that David wasn't the discoverer, he'd lose the limelight and the promotion that was sure to follow. The irony was that the peasant Zaya didn't even work for him. He was assigned to David by Sovereign Industries, which was under contract to structurally and facially restore the Forbidden City to its original grandeur. Sovereign Industries owned the building in which David worked; his company was merely a subcontractor.

Earlier in the day, David had approached Zaya and made him a deal—$1,000 for a written statement that David McAlister had made the discovery. Fortunately, the interpreter cared more about putting food on the family table than recognition, which would get him nothing more than a pat on the back. Once David put cash in the man's hand, there had been a rapid readjustment of Zaya's memory.

As David began typing an email to the president of the company, he detailed what had been found. He knew he'd piss off the several layers of management above him that he was bypassing with this breach of protocol, but he didn't care. Given half the chance, each of them would have done the same. His hands were flying across the keyboard, and he was at the point of explaining how his years of engineering experience had enabled him to piece together the clues that had led to this discovery, when he heard a metallic click. It was the sound the front door always made when the cipher lock released. He was sure he'd locked it after the last of his coworkers left for the day—but with so much on his mind, maybe not.

Standing, David looked across the sea of cubicles, hoping to get a glimpse of whoever had entered the office. "Hello," he yelled. No one responded. Perhaps whoever had entered had gone to the other side of the building and couldn't hear him. Or maybe he was just imagining things. He told himself to calm down. After all, he was on the thirtieth floor. Even if someone slipped past the security guard in the lobby, two codes were required to enter after hours—one for the building's elevator and another for the office. Only company employees and Sovereign's security manager had both.

Still, David had an unsettled feeling. Compounding his unease was the eerie glow of the full moon shining through the floor-to-ceiling windows, with the tinted glass dimming its brightness to such an extent that part of the office was cloaked in darkness. He was getting spooked. He wanted to turn on the overhead lights, but they were inoperative from ten o'clock in the evening until six in the morning. Management had jumped on the government's energy conservation bandwagon and placed timers on the lights.

Out of the corner of his eye, David thought he saw movement. But when he turned in that direction, there was only darkness. He was beginning to get more than a little freaked out. "Hello," he said again, this time cupping his hands around his mouth to better project his voice. But no one replied. He hoped he'd get a response from a cleaning person, or one of his coworkers who couldn't sleep and had decided to come in at this insane hour. Turning off the desk light, he dropped to his knees and crawled to the opposite side of the office, using the surrounding five-foot-high cubicle walls for cover and the thick pile carpet to mask the sound of his movement. When he reached the copy machine, which was in the farthest and darkest corner, he put his back to the wall and looked toward the moonlit windows. Sooner or later, he believed, the person who'd entered the office would pass in front of him.

David stared at the windows for a full ten minutes, saw no

one, and started to wonder if his imagination had gotten the better of him. Maybe he hadn't heard anyone. The noise could have been something as simple as a change in air pressure initiated by the building's air-conditioning system. Maybe that, in turn, had caused the door to move and pull against the lock. He chided himself for acting like a child and fearing the bogeyman. If he could gut it out for another fifteen minutes, he'd finish the email and be out of here.

Just as he started to return to his cubicle, David saw an enormous man, dressed entirely in black, cross the room three feet in front of him. Fortunately, despite being startled, he maintained his crouch and didn't move or make a sound. If he had, he'd have been face-to-face with an intruder who was at least six foot five and had to weigh several hundred pounds. David remained deathly still, held his breath, and followed the man with his eyes, avoiding any head movement that might draw attention. When the man passed beyond his peripheral vision, he slowly let out his breath. His hands and knees were shaking, and adrenaline was coursing through his body to such an extent that he thought his heart would explode. The office wasn't particularly large, so it was only a matter of time until he was discovered. The intruder clearly knew he was there, since he'd stupidly announced his presence—twice. He guessed that the giant was after corporate secrets, since it made little sense to break into an engineering firm just to ransack a few desks. David needed to call the security guard in the lobby and have him arrest the intruder. In fact, recalling the man's size, he'd tell the guard to send several security personnel and bring a Taser.

The nearest phone was in a cubicle twenty feet away. Moving slowly, David crawled into the eight-by-eight-foot space without making even the smallest sound. He pulled the wireless phone, at the corner of the desk, off its receptacle and dialed ★20, which would connect him with the guard in the lobby. As he was waiting for security to answer, he heard a noise coming from the vicinity of the copy machine. He quickly slid underneath the desk and pulled the chair in front of him. There was no answer from security. *What a time for a bathroom break.* David waited another minute, then redialed. The same result. He needed to get out of there.

Crawling from his hiding place, he hunched down as low as he could and duckwalked toward the office entrance, making sure to keep his head below the top of the cubicles. With the thick carpet absorbing his footsteps, he was confident the intruder didn't hear him. When he reached the lobby, he stood and pushed the door release button.

At that exact moment, a freight train hit David from behind. At least that's what it felt like. He was thrown across the lobby, landing so hard on his stomach that he nearly blacked out. As he started to regain his senses, powerful hands grabbed him by the shoulders and effortlessly lifted him off the floor. David found himself standing with his back to the intruder, an enormous forearm wrapped around his neck while a hand pushed his head forward so that he couldn't breathe. He tried to resist, repeatedly kicking the intruder in the shins as hard as he could to try to force him to release his stranglehold. Never flinching, the man maintained his viselike grip. David felt himself losing consciousness, and soon he collapsed motionless in the man's arms.

Kundek slung the engineer over his shoulder and carried him back to the cubicle where he'd been working, then lowered him into his chair. He removed a pair of latex gloves, a note, and a .22 handgun from his own pants pocket. Placing the engineer's hand around the grip of the gun and putting his finger on the trigger, just as he'd done with Batbayar, he pulled McAlister's finger back. The bullet entered the engineer's right temple and bounced around inside his cranium until it ran out of speed. Kundek let go of the body and changed gloves, since the ones he had been wearing were now covered with gunpowder residue.

Looking at the computer screen, he saw what David McAlister had been typing and erased it. He then searched through the computer files, looking for anything else he might need to purge. He found several photographs, downloaded them onto a flash drive he'd brought with him, then erased the folder they were in. Forty minutes after entering the building, he took the elevator down to the parking garage, walked out a side door, and was gone.

CHAPTER

2

Wang Lei sat behind his desk and listened to Kundek's descriptions of the killings. At five foot two inches tall, with a thin physique that displayed no body fat, the diminutive owner of Sovereign Industries didn't fit the mental image one might form of the most powerful and ruthless industrialist in China. Approaching sixty, he made sure his hair, which he kept short and combed straight back, remained black and that his face appeared young, thanks to Botox, periodic surgery, and his avoidance of the sun. He recognized that his vainness was well known and frequently made fun of behind his back, but he also knew that no one would ever dare comment about it to his face. Those few people who were indiscreet enough to do so no longer resided with the living.

As usual, Kundek had carried out his assignment perfectly. Batbayar Zaya and his wife were dead, killed by the same .22-caliber weapon that David McAlister had used to take his own life. At least that's what the official police report would say. The suicide note that the authorities would find on McAlister's desk had him confessing to the murders, explaining that Zaya had returned home early from a meeting and found McAlister in bed with Zaya's wife. Angry words had been exchanged, and Zaya had threatened to tell McAlister's employer about the affair. The note went on to say that after his confrontation with Zaya, McAlister had returned to his residence.

But then he had panicked, realizing that his indiscretion could get him fired and thus put him irrevocably behind in his spousal and child support payments. He had concluded that his only way out was to kill both Zaya and his wife and thus keep the affair a secret. However, unbeknownst to McAlister, a family friend whom he'd met before was staying at Zaya's residence. Upon hearing the gunshots, she had come out of the guest bedroom and seen McAlister standing over the bodies. She hadn't been in the house when he and Zaya's wife were making love earlier that evening, so she must have arrived after that. McAlister wrote that he was so surprised to see her that he froze, and that she ran out the front door and ducked between two residences before he could take a shot at her. He concluded his confession by acknowledging that he'd eventually be caught and that the penalty in China for his crime was death. Therefore, he had decided to spare himself a pointless trial, humiliation, and agony—and die on his own terms.

Wang had composed the suicide note and printed it out for Kundek to place next to the engineer's body. When found by the police, it would make for an open-and-shut case. Wang had to admit that he'd orchestrated everything quite well. McAlister's financial issues and marital history were common knowledge and formed the nexus of his plan. Wang didn't like the killings, because they could unintentionally bring undue attention to the most important undertaking of his life, but they had been a necessity. The irony was that Zaya's discovery had been initially unearthed by another worker two years earlier, and that worker, too, had been killed to protect the secret.

It had taken Wang quite some time to formulate his plan, which culminated when he obtained the cooperation of a very senior government official whose friendship he'd long cultivated. That person had an overwhelming desire to become president of China, but he was being forced by the Party to publicly announce his retirement. Although he'd never tell the official, Wang knew that the reason was that he lacked the requisite diplomatic skills for higher office.

Cautious in their discussions at first, because they were talking about treason, the official eventually became an eager participant in Wang's plan. If it had turned out that Wang had misjudged him or if the official had changed his mind, Wang would have sent Kundek to immediately resolve the situation. However, now that the second vice premier, the third most powerful person in China, was fully behind his operation, no one could prevent Wang from killing the presidents of the United States and China.

The Boeing 747-200B had 53,611 gallons of fuel in its tanks and was parked not far from its hangar, with two military personnel guarding the stairway leading to its forward port hatch. Twenty-six crew members were on board, along with sixty-nine of the seventy scheduled passengers. Matt Moretti was trying to get comfortable in a business–class–wide leather seat. As usual, his back was giving him problems, making it challenging for his six-foot-three, 230-pound body to find just the right position to stem the soreness. He didn't know how he'd do on the fourteen-hour flight if the pain worsened, especially since he'd recently given up drinking. But he was about to find out.

Looking at the high-profile people who sat near him, Moretti was amazed that he was with such an esteemed group. He'd been an Army Ranger until a helicopter crash in Afghanistan abruptly ended that career. It took a year of rehab just to regain his ability to walk, after which the army rewarded him with a pat on the back and a medical discharge. As a newly minted civilian, Moretti found it difficult to adjust to life outside the military, consuming large amounts of scotch ostensibly to lessen the continual pain in his back, when actually it was more about tuning out the world. He knew he was an alcoholic on a fast track to becoming another government mortality statistic—a discharged vet who'd tried and failed to adapt to civilian life. His self-destruction had been nearly complete when his friend Major Doug Cray, the only other survivor of the helicopter crash, helped straighten him out. Calling in some favors, Cray got Moretti a government job at the national archives in Anchorage. For the next five years, Cray served as counselor, therapist, and cheerleader in a healing process that eventually turned around the life of ex-Ranger Matt Moretti.

Less than a month ago, Moretti had been dealt another shitty blow when his sister was murdered in Venice. Traveling to Italy to escort her remains home, he had been approached by a Chinese agent, Han Li. In her late twenties, the stunning five-foot-eleven statuesque brunette had asked for his help in finding a series of documents that his sister had been working on just before her death. If made public, Han Li told Moretti, the revelations in those documents could result in the overthrow of her government. He initially turned down Han Li's request, until she offered him the one thing he couldn't refuse—the whereabouts of his sister's murderer. They had avoided death half a dozen times in the process of retrieving the documents, and then Han Li kept her word. On a dark night in a public square in Venice, Moretti had put a bullet in the center of the forehead of the man who had murdered his sister.

Moretti's exploits came to the attention of Colonel Vincent Pappas, commander of the Sixty-Sixth Military Intelligence Brigade in Wiesbaden, Germany. Impressed with Moretti's skill set, Pappas had summarily offered him a job as a civilian intelligence officer. That same day, Moretti had decided not to blow a good thing and gave up drinking. That was a month—and a lifetime—ago.

Moretti noticed a black Cadillac limousine approaching the Boeing 747's boarding ramp, flanked on either side by a Chevy Suburban. Then the Cadillac broke formation and pulled in front of the stairway leading to the plane's interior. Moretti knew the limousine was called the Beast, and he watched as its right rear passenger door opened. President John Ballinger exited the vehicle and walked briskly up the stairs into the aircraft. At that moment, an announcement came over the plane's intercom that the aircraft's call sign had changed from Air Force 29000 to Air Force One.

It was a moonless night. Two white cargo vans veered off the main expressway and turned onto a rutted dirt road that ascended a hill. The narrow strip of road, really just a pitted path cut through an area of dense foliage, passed close to the high walls and thick metal gates of mansions at intermittent intervals along the way. Kundek thought it strange, in an area where the residents were obviously wealthy, that the road wasn't paved. But then he concluded that these owners probably preferred a rough road so that motorists wouldn't be encouraged to use it as a shortcut between the two crowded thoroughfares. So they kept it unpaved, unlighted, and narrow, believing that was a small price to pay for privacy and seclusion in a city of sixteen million people.

The vans followed the path or road, whatever one wanted to call it, over the crest of the hill and down the other side. Eventually they stopped by a tall outgrowth of shrubbery, adjacent to which someone had spilled a can of luminescent orange paint. Kundek watched as four men exited his vehicle and five men the second, each wearing a large military-style backpack. The men all looked tough and walked with the practiced fluidity of professionals. Each group of men moved to the back of their respective van and removed a tall, green-metal tank on wheels from the cargo compartment.

Meanwhile Kundek walked into the dense shrubbery, shining his flashlight into the wall of green in front of him. The giant Mongolian seemed to be searching for something, moving his arm up and down and from side to side. Finally, he stopped and pushed the palm of his hand forward. Almost immediately there was an audible click, followed by the sound of stone rubbing against stone. Standing within the shrubbery, Kundek used his thick fingers to pull open a five-foot-high, three-foot-wide slate door, which had sprung forward from the wall when he pushed a slight protuberance in the rock.

The thirty-six-inch-wide door within the shrubbery was just wide enough for eight men, along with their two metal tanks and huge backpacks, to squeeze through. Once they were inside the opening, the remaining two men adjusted the shrub in front of the wall so that it appeared undisturbed, removed the orange paint from the dirt, and brushed the footprints and tire tracks from the metal tanks off the dirt road. Then they got into the two vans and drove away.

Moretti reclined his chair and was deep into the latest Michael Connelly book when a Secret Service agent tapped him on the shoulder.

"President Ballinger would like to see you, sir."

Moretti looked up at the agent, who was conservatively dressed in a dark blue suit and light blue tie, and put down his book. As he got up, a stabbing pain flashed across his back and he momentarily stumbled. The Secret Service agent offered his hand in assistance, but it was refused. Moretti limped for a few steps and then, as the pain lessened, began to walk normally. He followed the agent to the forward part of the aircraft, passing through several layers of security before stopping outside a door that bore the presidential seal.

The agent escorting him knocked once and, when he heard a voice telling them to enter, opened the door to the president's private office. The president of the United States, who was seated behind his desk, got up as soon as he saw Moretti. He directed him to a couch and took a seat beside him.

"Would you like something to drink?" the president asked as a steward silently appeared at the door and waited for instructions.

"Just water."

Ballinger held up two fingers, and the steward left and closed the door behind him.

The chief executive of the United States was a widower, his wife having succumbed five years earlier to breast cancer. He wasn't tall, nor did he have the movie idol good looks of Ronald Regan. He stood five ten, was neither fat nor skinny, and had dark brown hair generously sprinkled with gray. His demeanor was that of a Midwesterner, which meant he was down to earth and true to his word. If asked, he'd say he absorbed these qualities while growing up in the small town of Salina, Kansas.

The president was familiar with Moretti's drinking problem and admired him for having the courage to overcome his addiction. He wished that some in his administration—and more than a few in Congress—would follow his example. They exchanged small talk until the steward brought them each a glass of water and departed.

Then President Ballinger began. "I believe someone from my office told you that we've been invited to the gala, as the Chinese government refers to it, celebrating the six-hundredth anniversary of the Forbidden City? It's being held on the night we arrive, and we'll be the only two foreigners in attendance."

"Yes, sir," said Moretti. "And if you don't mind me saying so, this function seems well beyond my GS-12 pay grade."

"If it hadn't been for you, I wouldn't have been invited. I'm the tagalong. There's a long list of heads of state who wanted to come to this event and suck up to our hosts, but the Chinese turned them down flat. President Liu wanted the gala to be a domestic celebration of his country's cultural heritage, without the baggage of dealing with foreign dignitaries and their hidden agendas. We're here because he wanted to personally thank you for helping retrieve the lost documents of Chairman Mao. He realizes that if you hadn't, he'd no longer be in office. You saved his ass."

The look on Moretti's face suggested that he was embarrassed by the praise.

"However, truth be known," continued the president, "there's a second reason for the invitation. But before I get into that, I want you to understand that everything I tell you stays between us and the two other parties whom I'll mention."

"That's a given, Mr. President."

"That being said, are you familiar with the Chinese industrialist Wang Lei?"

"Only from the intelligence briefs I've read," said Moretti. "He's one of the wealthiest men in China. He's vain, has a huge ego, is very nationalistic, owns the only nongovernment defense contracting company in the country, and advocates that China's military should start fighting its enemies beyond its borders."

"A good summary, but let me add to what you already know. When Mao Zedong came to power in 1949, he modeled China's defense industry, along with almost everything else, on that of the Soviet Union. Centralization was the order of the day. The government—or more accurately, the Chinese Communist Party—assumed ownership of every business, which all became state-owned enterprises or SOEs. They were set up not to be efficient, but to employ vast numbers of workers so that unemployment would be low. The Party thought that if people had jobs, and thus could feed their families and cover the basic expenses of their everyday lives, they would believe the government was looking out for them and not demand a democratic form of government. However, employing such massive numbers of people also meant that SOEs were bloated with excess workers. As a result, they were inefficient, rarely made money, and became rife with corruption. Moreover, no matter how hard a person worked, everything belonged to the state. You get the picture?"

Moretti said he did, and the president continued.

"The SOEs that manufactured armaments, for example,

couldn't produce the required quantity or quality of military hardware demanded of them. During that time, Wang Lei was employed as a senior manager in a munitions factory, a position that he obtained because his late father had been a friend of Chairman Mao. As a result, Wang was given a seat on the gravy train. The job description for people in those positions consisted of showing up for work, collecting their money on payday, embezzling just enough from the budget not to be considered greedy, and leaving for home whenever they wanted. But Wang was a die-hard nationalist who didn't subscribe to any of those practices. Nor did he believe that the government's policy of making cheap copies of armaments manufactured by America, Europe, and the Soviet Union would build China's defense industry. Are you following me so far?"

"I am, Mr. President, but what allowed Wang to become the only nongovernment defense contractor in China?"

"He turned to an old family friend, Jiang Zemin, who had risen from mayor of Shanghai to the leader of China. Over the years, they'd frequently discussed the benefits of having a private defense manufacturing company that could operate with fewer employees and turn a profit, since the government's massive subsidies to SOEs were steadily draining the economy."

"And Jiang contacted Wang Lei once he took over the top spot," Moretti added.

"That's what we believe," confirmed the president. "However it happened, Jiang issued a government charter authorizing the industrialist's company as a defense contractor. The only stipulation was that all manufactured arms had to be sold to the Chinese military. Jiang initially got some pushback from the Defense Ministry for his actions, but that faded quickly when he assured officials that they'd be allowed to keep their positions. Over the next twenty-three years, Wang's company, Sovereign Industries, grew at an astonishing rate. It's now the major supplier of advanced weaponry to the Chinese military, and it's so important to national security that the government doesn't want to mess with it. What that means is that they don't want to split the company into smaller units or issue another license."

"Does Sovereign Industries somehow affect the security of the United States?" asked Moretti.

"President Liu and I believe it does. We think Wang Lei is selling arms outside of China, in violation of his mandate. If he is, we need to know who's buying them. These are satellite images of one of Wang's manufacturing plants, which produces cruise missiles, along with photos of two adjacent warehouses. They were taken two weeks ago," the president said as he reached behind him and took a folder off his desk. He selected three eight-by-ten photos and handed them to Moretti.

The images looked like someone had taken x-rays of the interiors of several buildings. One photo clearly showed row after row of cruise missiles on a manufacturing line. The other two eight-by-tens were of warehouses in which missiles were stored from one end to the other.

"These two photos were taken three days ago," the president said, handing Moretti the last photos from the folder.

"Everything's gone," Moretti said, stating the obvious. "Both warehouses are now empty."

"The question is, where did all those missiles go? When I confronted President Liu about whether he was sending missiles to another government, he denied it. That doesn't necessarily mean anything; in the world of politics, lying to protect your country's secrets is the norm. But I'm certain that he believed I had documented proof, or I wouldn't have been asking."

"Do you believe him?"

"Yes. I served two terms as governor of Kansas and one as its senator. My bullshit meter is pretty good. Liu's in the dark. And if that's true, it could be bad news for the United States. Even if the buyer doesn't use these missiles to attack our homeland, they can still be fired at our embassies, overseas bases, or anywhere else Americans congregate."

"Sir, China isn't a democracy. Can't President Liu have the government take over Wang Lei's company or replace him as CEO, in the interest of national security?"

"Not without solid proof, and I'm not about to turn over these photos," said President Ballinger. "But President Liu has other problems as well. Thanks to his strong reputation in the defense sector, Wang Lei enjoys a great deal of support from ranking government officials—the same bureaucrats who will determine whether President Liu is allowed to serve a second five-year term. Moreover, taking a heavy hand against a well-respected businessman, especially one who has never succumbed to the corruption around him, would not sit well with most Chinese. Wang Lei is also admired as a patron of China's heritage because he has helped to restore his country's national treasures, including the Forbidden City, which also endears him to the general population. Unless we can provide President Liu with incontrovertible proof that Wang Lei has broken the law, the man's untouchable."

"And how am I involved, sir?"

"I want to be clear that what I'm proposing is very dangerous," said the president.

"Sir?"

"Since you and Han Li will both be going to the gala, President Liu and I thought that would be a perfect opportunity to bring the team together again, so to speak. We want the two of you to find out where those missiles were sent. This is strictly a volunteer assignment. If you don't want to do it, now's the time to let me know."

"That never crossed my mind, Mr. President."

"Apparently Han Li said the same thing to President Liu. You're definitely cut from the same cloth."

"When do we start, sir?"

"The day after the gala. Since you and Han Li are honored guests, you'd be missed before then. President Liu and I believe that Wang Lei would keep sensitive information, such as the names of buyers of his arms, under tight control. Since he spends most of his time in his office, that's the first place you'll look. However, if it's not there, then do whatever you have to do to find the location of those missiles."

The president took a sip of water before he continued. "If you're caught by Wang or his men, no one will help you. You'll almost certainly be tortured for whatever information they can beat or waterboard out of you and then killed. If they do decide to let you live and hand you over to Chinese authorities, which is unlikely, you'll be considered criminals and sentenced for the break-in. If that happens, you can expect two decades at hard labor. Do you understand?"

Moretti said he did.

The president stood and walked to the door, indicating that their meeting was over. "No one will say thank you for what you're about to do because only a few people know about it. But I'm saying it now." With that, the president extended his hand, which Moretti quickly accepted.

President Liu was waiting at the bottom of the stairs and greeted President Ballinger as he stepped off Air Force One. After inspecting the military honor guard in front of the VIP terminal at the Beijing International Airport, they both made short speeches to the world press. Then they posed for photographs and were escorted to separate cars in a forty-vehicle motorcade. While that was happening, the passengers and crew disembarked and made their way to one of two buses going to the St. Regis Hotel, near the American embassy on the east side of the city.

The last passenger off the plane, Moretti was headed to the second bus when someone grabbed his arm. Instinctively turning toward his aggressor, he came face-to-face with a tall Asian woman in her late twenties. She had porcelain-like skin, an athletic build, long brunette hair, and black opal-colored eyes. Han Li was a head turner.

"Just who I was looking for," Moretti said. "Care to join me for a bus ride to the St. Regis?"

Han Li replied, "President Liu upgraded your accommodations. You're spending the night, along with your president and other Chinese dignitaries, in the Forbidden City."

"That sounds like an offer I can't refuse. How are we getting there?"

Han Li pointed to a black Audi A5, which was six vehicles from the rear of the motorcade.

"I didn't know the Forbidden City had a hotel on-site," Moretti said, after placing his carry-on bag in the trunk and getting into the passenger seat.

"It doesn't. In preparation for the gala, President Liu asked the contractor to install running water, sanitary facilities, and lighting in some of the palaces and buildings, as long as it wouldn't destroy or deface any part of the structure. To accommodate his request, the engineers installed chemical toilets, underground water tanks, and battery-powered lighting."

Before Moretti could ask another question, the presidential convoy started to move. Han Li kept half a car length between her Audi and the SUV she was following.

Beijing's traffic was horrendous, particularly in the area around the Forbidden City, which is at the foot of Tiananmen Square. To address that problem, the military had blocked off the inside lane of the main highway by setting up concrete barriers on either side, thereby isolating the convoy's route. The result was that what would normally have been a one-hour drive took only twenty minutes. During that time, Moretti and Han Li shared what each knew about Wang Lei, then discussed the best way to break into his offices without ending up on a medical examiner's table.

Soon the Forbidden City came into view, and Han Li took the opportunity to share some of its history with Moretti. Built between 1406 and 1420, the Forbidden City had been the residence of twenty-four emperors. Within the 178-acre compound, which was surrounded by 33-foot-high walls and a 170-foot-wide and 20-foot-deep moat, there were ninety palaces and courtyards, 980 buildings, and 8,704 rooms. From their approach, Moretti could see the Tiananmen Gate, which Han Li told him was the main entry into the compound. There were three additional entrances, each facing a cardinal compass direction, but those were blocked for security purposes.

When the convoy stopped, both presidents exited their vehicles and waved to the tens of thousands of people who'd gathered to see the heads of state. After the presidents and their security details entered the compound, everyone else followed in a prearranged pecking order. Luggage was placed on carts and taken to a separate inspection station, where each bag was opened and examined before being taken to its owner's overnight residence. Han Li and Moretti each had a carry-on, which was taken from them, inspected, and placed on a cart for eventual delivery to their room. Moretti assumed the baggage would also undergo chemical or biological inspections, possibly both, before being released to them later that day.

Moretti and Han Li were the last to approach the guest inspection stations, having waited patiently until the other invitees and their security details went through. To gain entrance, a person had to undergo three separate security checks. The first was a facial recognition scan, which compared the person's face to their national ID card photo stored in the government's database. In Moretti's case, the US State Department had previously sent his passport photo to China's foreign minister for inclusion in their system.

The second security station was an x-ray machine, similar in appearance to those found in major airports. The difference, however, was that this equipment was decidedly more powerful and didn't care one bit about a person's right to privacy. The image viewed by security staff in an adjacent area left nothing to the imagination.

At the last station were technicians who took swabs of a person's clothing and skin to feed into on-site sensors, testing for trace amounts of explosive residue and a plethora of known harmful pathogens. Both presidents and the senior vice premier, the second-most powerful person in China, bypassed these stations.

Once cleared, Moretti and Han Li each were fingerprinted and had a digital image of their retinas taken. They were then issued identification badges attached to lanyards, which they were told to keep visible at all times.

After passing through security, they set off at a brisk pace toward their quarters. Around them, as best as Moretti could estimate, several thousand serious-faced Chinese military, each carrying an automatic weapon, were looking for the security cards dangling from the lanyards around their necks.

Just outside the area where everyone would be spending the night, and where the gala would be held, they encountered another security checkpoint, this one defined by an eight-foot-high metal fence that bisected the Forbidden City. In front of this barrier was a line of People's Liberation Army soldiers standing shoulder to shoulder. Han Li and Moretti approached the entrance gate and presented their ID cards, after which scans of their retinas and fingerprints were electronically compared with those stored in the database. Once verified, they were permitted to proceed into the Inner Court section of the compound.

Han Li explained that President Liu was spending the night in the Palace of Heavenly Purity, while President Ballinger would be in the Palace of Earthly Tranquility, both of which she pointed out to Moretti. She told him that these palaces, formerly used by emperors of China, had not been occupied for more than a century. Connecting the two structures was the Hall of Union, where the senior vice premier, as well as various heads of Chinese ministries, would be residing. Moretti, Han Li, and several lower-level government officials would be staying to the west of these buildings, in the Hall of Mental Cultivation. Junior government officials, staff members, and security personnel would be relegated to other structures throughout the Inner Court.

Moretti and Han Li were five minutes from their rooms, and adjacent to the Palace of Earthly Tranquility, when Moretti's cell phone rang. When he finished his conversation, he turned to Han Li and said, "President Ballinger wants to meet before the gala. A Secret Service agent is coming to escort us through security."

Han Li asked, "Why would he want to meet me?"

"I guess we're about to find out. I told the agent where we are."

Soon they saw a Caucasian man in a dark blue business suit headed straight for them. He was six foot eight, with jet-black hair parted on the left and the square-jawed sternness of someone who did not mince words. He introduced himself as Jack Bonaquist, special agent in charge of the president's protective division. Moretti had spoken to him briefly on board Air Force One, when both were in the galley getting coffee. Moretti and Han Li were given visitor badges, then escorted into the Palace of Earthly Tranquility and through several layers of Secret Service agents, eventually arriving at a room at the rear of the palace. Bonaquist knocked on the door, and the president told him to enter.

Moretti stopped in his tracks upon seeing the leader of the free world standing before him dressed in attire from another century. The president was wearing a black worsted, swallowtail, satin-trimmed coat with matching trousers. Underneath he had on a French-cuffed white shirt with black studs down the center and a white vest. Each cuff was attached by a dull-black cuff link with the presidential seal emblazoned on it. A white bow tie, black silk top hat, white gloves, and patent leather oxford shoes with spats finished the distinctive look.

The president smiled when he saw the surprise on Moretti's face. "Not what you expected?"

"Not exactly, sir."

"And this must be Han Li," President Ballinger said, walking to her and extending his hand, which she quickly accepted. "I wanted to meet the other half of the team that President Liu and I are sending on such an important and perilous assignment. After reading about your performance in Venice, I'm a great admirer."

Han Li looked embarrassed, something Moretti had never thought possible.

Just then the door to the room opened, and President Liu entered wearing the yellow court robes of the emperor of China.

His garments were embellished with gold, pearls, and what looked to be precious stones arranged in various intricate patterns.

"It's a pleasure to finally meet you, Mr. Moretti," President Liu said as he walked over and shook his hand. "My country owes you an enormous debt of gratitude for your heroism in Venice."

"Thank you, sir, but most of the credit goes to Han Li."

President Liu bowed his head slightly in her direction as a sign of respect, and then returned his attention to Moretti. "Your humility is very Chinese. I hope you and Miss Li will enjoy this evening's celebration. Without the perseverance and heroics you both displayed, I assure you this event would not have occurred. Now, if you'll excuse me, I have several matters that require my attention before the festivities." He then turned and said his farewell to President Ballinger, who escorted him to the door.

"I know you both think we're crazy," the president said as he returned to Han Li and Moretti. "But everyone this evening, except for myself and our security details, will be in period dress from the fifteenth-century Ming dynasty. We'll eat and drink as if we were in the court of the emperor of China. Your attire is in your rooms. I'll be the only exception to the dress code. President Liu and I both agree that if I wore period clothing, the world press would speculate, or flat out fabricate, stories that I've now subjugated United States trade and economic policy to the dictates of the Chinese. Therefore, you're looking at what the president of the United States might have worn to a formal event at the beginning of the last century. Now, as time is running short, if you'll both excuse me, I have a few things to do before the gala."

When they left the room, Bonaquist was waiting outside the door to escort them from the building, after which he took back their visitor badges. "The Hall of Mental Cultivation, where you both will be housed, is just to the west of where President Liu is staying," he said, pointing them in the right direction. Moretti thanked him, and he and Han Li started toward their rooms.

It took only five minutes to walk to their housing, the former residence of eight Chinese emperors. They found their luggage in each of their rooms and, spread across their beds, the period clothing mentioned by the president. On top was a diagram of the building and directions to the gala. Moretti picked up the drawing and saw that the throne and reception rooms were in the front portion of the building and that their section contained several small bedrooms.

Deciding to wash up, and expecting to find a bathroom and shower, he opened the door at the back of his room. Instead he entered a closet-like enclosure containing only a chemical toilet, similar to a portable restroom. Disappointed, but understanding that the Chinese government wanted to keep their alterations to the ancient structure to a minimum, he walked back into the bedroom. That's when he noticed a pitcher of water, a porcelain basin, and two towels sitting on a small table to the right of the bathroom door. As a former Army Ranger, Moretti was no stranger to a cold shave. He cleaned up, got dressed, and was about to go across the hall and check on his partner when he heard a knock on his door.

Opening the door, he saw Han Li standing before him wearing a form-fitting *qipao*—a one-piece, dark blue, high-collared dress that extended from her neck to her toes. Accentuating her long legs and sensational five-foot-eleven athletic physique, a generous slit extended up the right side of the dress to her hip. Moretti wore a black *changshan*, the looser-fitting male equivalent of the qipao, but with a collar and lacking the slit.

"You look ravishing," Moretti said, unable to take his eyes off her.

Han Li didn't reply, but the look on her face told him that she was pleased with the way he was looking at her.

They left the building and walked to the northeastern section of the Forbidden City, where the gala was being held in the courtyard of the Palace of Tranquil Longevity. After their retinal image and fingerprints were verified, and following a pat-down, they were allowed to enter. The courtyard, half the size of a football field, was bordered by tall trees whose broad leafy limbs provided a magnificent green canopy. Candles and lanterns gave the entire area an elegant glow.

Moretti had just lifted a glass of water off the tray of a passing waiter, when a roll of drums announced that both chiefs of state, with President Liu slightly ahead, had entered the courtyard. The silence was immediate as everyone except Moretti bowed, but he quickly followed suit upon realizing that he was the only person standing erect. A moment later, President Liu said something in Chinese, which Moretti guessed was the equivalent of "Let the party begin," and the noise and conversations returned.

The weather was perfect, cool but not cold, and although he had no idea what he was eating, Moretti found the food superb. He had wanted to use the occasion to spend some time with Han Li, but she had a group of admirers who didn't seem to want to let her out of their sight. Just as Moretti thought about breaking in and asking her to dance, an elderly Chinese man approached Han Li. Her group of male suitors immediately departed, and the two of them became an item for the rest of the evening.

The man appeared to be in his seventies, stood six feet tall, and carried a slight gut. His hair was black, as was the hair of every other Chinese person at the gala. Moretti found himself a little jealous of the septuagenarian who was monopolizing Han Li's time. He thought about barging in on their conversation, but decided against it since the two of them seemed to be enjoying each other's company.

Both presidents departed shortly after midnight, and Han Li's elderly friend left at twelve thirty. Then Han Li found Moretti and they walked together back to their quarters. They agreed to meet at eight o'clock the next morning, after which she'd drive him to the St. Regis Hotel to check in. Then they'd decide on the best way to break into Wang's office.

As he returned to his room, Moretti was jet-lagged and looking forward to getting a good night's sleep. Unfortunately his good night's sleep ended at just six o'clock, when all hell broke loose.

CHAPTER

4

Moretti heard someone pounding on his door, but he believed he was having a dream until three Chinese soldiers barged into his room. One pointed a rifle at him, while the others searched the bedroom and bathroom. When they were done, they left without a word of explanation. He was putting on his clothes when Han Li came through his open doorway.

"What's going on?" Moretti asked. The look on Han Li's face warned him that the answer was not going to be good.

"One of the guards told me," she said, "that President Ballinger, President Liu, the senior vice premier, and three senior government officials are missing."

Moretti stared at Han Li in disbelief. With the security he'd seen, he had difficulty believing what she'd just told him. "How's that possible? There's an army of soldiers inside and outside the Forbidden City, and wall-to-wall Secret Service agents surrounding the president. An anorexic cockroach couldn't sneak through."

"Nevertheless, no one can find them," said Han Li.

"Let me see what I can find out from the Secret Service," Moretti said as he finished putting on his shoes. He thought that flying on Air Force One and being invited to the gala was going to cut him some slack with the Secret Service, but he was mistaken. As far as they were concerned, Moretti was a civilian intelligence officer stationed in Germany—not in their chain of command and with no need to know, which in government parlance meant that whatever was going on was none of his business.

When Moretti and Han Li met back at the Inner Court, she reported similar luck with the Chinese military commander, Lieutenant Colonel Yan He. As they were discussing what they should do next, they were approached by the older man with whom Han Li had spent time at the gala. She introduced him to Moretti as Gao Hui, a close friend of her late uncle and a member of the most powerful decision-making body in China, the Politburo Standing Committee.

"How could this happen?" Han Li asked, looking at the multitude of soldiers and Secret Service agents around them.

"That is indeed the operative question," Gao replied.

"We'd like to help," said Han Li, "but neither the American Secret Service nor Yan He seems to want to give us the time of day."

"I believe the lieutenant colonel and the soldiers who were on duty are very worried about going to prison for dereliction of duty. They don't want outside help, because if anyone except them succeeds in uncovering vital clues or discovering what has happened, they'll look even more incompetent. I imagine the Secret Service has somewhat the same belief. Losing a president is not an endorsement of one's competency."

"That's an understatement," Moretti said.

Taking Han Li by the arm, Gao led her and Moretti back in the direction from which they had come. "If you and Mr. Moretti would like to have a look inside the palaces where the presidents were staying," Gao told Han Li, "as well as the buildings from which the government officials seem to be missing, I may be able to help."

"That would be greatly appreciated," Han Li replied.

"Are the buildings all close together?" Moretti asked as they started toward the Palace of Earthly Tranquility, where President Ballinger had been staying.

"No," said Gao, "only the residences for President Liu, President Ballinger, and Senior Vice Premier Chen Gaoli are near each other. The others, from which the three government officials are missing, are in an area referred to as the eastern palaces."

"Who were the government officials?" Han Li asked.

"Tang Ji, minister of national defense; Dai Shao, minister of state security; and Yu Quan, minister of commerce."

"And how many ministers and others spent the night in the Inner Court?" she continued.

"Sixty-seven Party and city officials, twenty of whom are ministers, spent the night in refurbished quarters within the Forbidden City," Gao replied.

Moretti wondered what was unique about the three missing ministers. He understood taking both presidents and even the senior vice premier, which would give whoever apparently abducted them tremendous leverage in negotiations. But why take ministers who would seem to be insignificant in any negotiation? Another thing that puzzled him was that the eastern palaces were nowhere near the presidents' quarters, which meant that whoever kidnapped the three ministers had been willing to accept that exponentially higher degree of risk. Apparently having the presidents and the senior vice premier was not enough to complete their objective. Again, why?

They arrived at the security perimeter established by the Secret Service, where four agents stood guard, barring entrance into the Palace of Earthly Tranquility. One look at the face of the agent who came forward told Moretti that no amount of talk or coercion was going to persuade him to let them inside. That was confirmed when he was told in no uncertain terms to take a hike.

Grasping at a straw, Moretti asked to speak with Bonaquist. Obviously surprised that Moretti knew the head of the presidential detail, the agent summoned Bonaquist on his hand mic. He apparently didn't want to risk pissing off his boss by sending away someone who might be a friend.

Several minutes later, Bonaquist appeared. "We're kind of busy, Moretti. What do you want?" he asked in a voice that expressed a combination of weariness, impatience, and irritability.

"We'd like to have a look inside the palace to see if we can help," Moretti said.

"No," Bonaquist replied, turning around to leave.

Just then Gao Hui called to him, "Agent Bonaquist, my government would like to understand what's happened. Our president and four government officials are missing. This palace belongs to the sovereign state of China. You and your men are here only as guests."

Upon hearing this stern admonition, Bonaquist turned around and looked at Gao, who held up his credentials.

Han Li spoke up and said, "He's a member of the Politburo Standing Committee, the most senior government body in our country."

Looking at Bonaquist, Moretti knew what was almost certainly going through the agent's mind. Gao was right—Bonaquist had no authority to keep the Chinese government from entering the palace. If he tried to do so, it could get ugly and cause an incident, which was the last thing the agent wanted since his own president was also missing.

The head of the presidential detail took a deep breath and said to Gao, "It would be my pleasure, sir, to escort you inside."

Entering the palace, Bonaquist led them to what had been the president's quarters. The flooring, platform surrounding the emperor's throne, interior walls, and various sections of the ceiling had been torn apart. As a result, there wasn't much to see except a room filled with debris.

"Quite a mess," Gao said.

Bonaquist didn't respond, feeling sheepish at the damage that he and his men had inflicted on what was obviously a national treasure.

"Did you find anything?" Moretti asked.

"Nothing. I'd have been surprised if we had," said Bonaquist. "We have a very strict series of protocols on how we inspect rooms and buildings in which the president will be staying. Those procedures were followed to the letter."

"Can I ask what you look for?" said Gao.

Picking up on Moretti's desire to help, Bonaquist adopted a more cooperative demeanor. "Before the president arrives, we secure the area in which he'll be staying. Immediately thereafter we conduct an extensive electronic and sensor probe of the premises, both inside and out. We look for listening devices, hidden passageways, cameras, monitors, explosives, biological and chemical agents, and anything else that could affect his privacy or security. We then x-ray the walls, floors, and ceiling. Once that is complete, we use ground-penetrating radar, or GPR, to look under concrete and other seemingly impenetrable surfaces that our x-ray machines can't completely penetrate."

Pointing to where they'd entered, Bonaquist added, "That door is the only way in or out of this room. It's under constant video monitoring, and we have two agents standing in front of it at all times."

Gao asked, "And no one entered or left the room from the time the president went to bed until it was discovered that he was missing?"

"No one. I personally reviewed that video recording from last night to this morning. I can tell you that my agents were awake and alert at all times, and that the imagery was not being looped. The president entered this room at twenty minutes past midnight, and no one opened that door until six this morning when one of our agents entered to bring him breakfast."

"He couldn't just disappear," Moretti said.

"Don't you think I know that? If he didn't open that door," Bonaquist said, again pointing to the only entrance to the room, "then this room must, by definition, have a secret exit—or so I believed. But as you can see, we've ripped out the floor and there's just hard-packed dirt underneath. This morning we again ran the GPR across it and it's solid. We know there's no trapdoor or crawl space in the walls because, as you can see, we tore them apart and found no openings. We even took apart the platform surrounding the throne," he said, pointing to the corner of the room where only a spindly four-legged chair, covered in purple silk, sat. "There's nothing but hard-packed dirt below. We then ripped apart the ceiling and the roof above this room, looking for an exit or entry point. Nada."

Moretti glanced up at the blue sky above him.

"Yeah," admitted Bonaquist, "the Chinese are going to be real pleased with our carpentry skills when they see what we've done."

"You're being far more open with us than I expected," Moretti said.

"I want you and your friend from the Chinese government," said Agent Bonaquist, "to know that we tore this place apart looking for tunnels, doorways, secret passageways, hidden spaces, and any other method you could imagine for someone to gain entry and leave unseen. I also ordered both guards who were posted outside the president's door to take a blood test for any foreign substance that might have been introduced into their systems. Their medical tests came back negative. Our techs, who are on loan from the NSA, are the best on the planet. They tell me they're certain that no one hacked into our external or internal security cameras."

Han Li and Gao Hui looked as astonished as Moretti, who said, "Given what you've told me, what just happened seems impossible."

"Even more so since it occurred five more times," said Bonaquist. "The Chinese had similar security screenings and protection details in place for President Liu, the second vice premier, and their three ministers."

Then Bonaquist took a deep breath and stepped close to

Moretti. "Look, I heard what you and Han Li did in Venice." Surprised, Moretti was about to respond when Bonaquist held up his hand and added, "We guard the president, but we're not deaf. Putting my ego aside, I could frankly use your help—yours and Han Li's."

"It would be our pleasure," said Moretti.

Then Moretti, Han Li, and Gao left and headed for the Palace of Heavenly Purity and then to the buildings from where the others had been kidnapped. Just as Bonaquist had described, the Chinese military had also conducted extensive x-ray and GPR scanning of every surface within and below those buildings. And despite tearing apart the buildings in the same manner as the Secret Service, they had found not a single clue.

Finally Gao Hui left for his office, and Moretti and Han Li started walking back toward their rooms. "Let's go over what we know, which is almost nothing," Moretti suggested. "The abductions—which others may call kidnappings—occurred, as Agent Bonaquist pointed out, sometime between twelve twenty and six o'clock this morning. According to Gao, everyone who was abducted had a panic button that, when pressed, would bring an armed response to their rooms in an instant."

"Therefore," Han Li said, "whoever abducted them must have done it while they were asleep. It happened so quickly that no one had time to press their alarm."

"Exactly. Did you also notice that the presidents' watches and everyone's cell phones were left behind?"

"I noticed that," Han Li replied. "I understand the cell phones because they could be used as tracking devices, but why the watches?"

"Because they work in conjunction with the subdermal tracking devices inserted under the skin of each president. Whoever kidnapped the presidents knew about the devices and how they could be neutralized."

"They might know, but I don't. Explain it to me," Han Li

said as they walked into the Hall of Mental Cultivation and went to Moretti's room.

"The tracking device is a small silicon chip inserted under the skin," explained Moretti, "but it doesn't have the power to transmit over any meaningful distance. Instead, it relies on an external device to boost its signal so that it can be picked up by government monitoring equipment. That relay transmitter is usually contained in a cell phone or watch."

"How do you know all this?"

"Some of the people with whom I work in Europe are potential kidnapping targets, so they have these chips inserted in themselves. My unit is one of several that have the equipment necessary to receive and track that signal."

"And since the watches and cell phones have been left behind, the signals are too weak to detect," said Han Li.

"Precisely."

"It's as if they were sucked into a black hole."

"A black hole?" asked Moretti.

Han Li started to explain, "Yes, a black hole is ..."

"I know what it is," Moretti interrupted, "and I think you're on to something."

"I was being metaphorical."

"I'm not." Moretti went to the nightstand and picked up a floor plan of the Hall of Mental Cultivation, which had earlier been left with his period clothing. He studied it for a few seconds, and then bolted from the room.

"Where are you going?" Han Li yelled.

"Follow me!"

Han Li caught up with Moretti as he entered the Throne Room, which had been used by the emperor to conduct state affairs and hold private audiences. There were dozens of similar areas scattered throughout the Forbidden City, all in locations personally favored by the various rulers of China. Each throne was unique in design and rested against a wall or barrier, undoubtedly so that no one could come up behind the emperor and surprise him.

Moretti checked the back of the throne, which was securely fastened to the inside wall. Then he went outside and checked the exterior wall behind the throne, finding it solid with no hidden passageway into the building.

When he came back inside, Han Li was standing next to the throne. "Did you find anything?" she asked.

"Not a blessed thing, but it has to be here."

"*What* has to be here?"

Moretti didn't answer. Instead, he slowly ran his hand over the throne's ornate wooden surface, as if frisking it for contraband. There appeared to be nothing unusual in what essentially was a chair—no hidden compartments or secret levers. After nearly three quarters of an hour, he was at the exact same place as a plethora of Secret Service agents and their counterparts in the People's Liberation Army—absolutely nowhere.

Moretti's back was starting to spasm, and he needed to lie down, stretch, and rest for a moment to keep it from locking up. He found a flat spot beside the throne and tried to bring his knee up to his chest, but that hurt too much. Instead, he stretched out flat and closed his eyes, waiting for the spasms to subside. Ten minutes later, he looked up and saw Han Li standing over him.

"Feel any better?" she asked.

"Not a hundred percent, but it'll have to do." Moretti clenched his teeth, anticipating the pain, and rolled over on his stomach before raising himself to a kneeling position. Just as he was about to stand up, he saw an almost imperceptible bulge in the fabric beneath the throne. If it hadn't been at eye level, he never would have noticed the irregularly shaped area. Pulling away the silk fabric, he discovered a three-inch-long lever. Gently tugging at it until it released, he pulled it toward him and heard two distinct *clicks*. At the base of the throne, both metal braces attaching the right side of the throne to a wooden block had released, whereas the left braces remained in place. He pushed the emperor's seat of power aside until it came to rest at a forty-five-degree angle, revealing an opening in the center of the wooden block.

"I think we could use those emergency flashlights," Moretti said, pointing to the corner of the room where two were cradled in charging units attached to the wall.

Han Li handed him a flashlight, and he directed the light into the opening. The first thing he saw was a disintegrating bamboo ladder descending seven feet to the floor of a tunnel, which then made a ninety-degree turn in the direction of the outside wall. Remembering that each person who'd been kidnapped had slept in a structure that had a throne room, Moretti now understood how someone had gained access into those highly protected spaces. This also explained why neither government had detected the presence of a tunnel, even with the most sophisticated equipment. Since the throne rested against the wall, the opening would have been revealed only if the x-ray or GPR was positioned directly above it. Except for the shaft extending vertically from under the throne seat, the tunnel was outside the footprint of the building.

Asking Han Li to shine her light into the opening, Moretti put his flashlight in his pocket and grabbed a bamboo pole in each hand. Avoiding the decomposing rungs of the ladder, he slid down the six-hundred-year-old stalks. "Come down and join me," he yelled up to Han Li when he reached the floor of the tunnel. "But make sure you pull the throne back into position before you descend. We need to keep what we've found to ourselves, at least for the moment."

Han Li grabbed a bamboo stalk with one hand and pulled the throne chair back into position with the other. After hearing a satisfying double click, she descended.

A little more than eight feet in diameter, the inside of the tunnel was faced with small, hand-sized pieces of porcelain, which appeared to be arranged in intricate geometric patterns. Over the centuries some pieces had come loose and fallen, and those that remained attached were mostly covered with grime. The air was dense and musty, which made it difficult to breathe. Moretti believed this was because the tunnel was still relatively well sealed, which meant that the oxygen level would be low. If they weren't careful, they could easily become asphyxiated before they realized it. Another problem was that they were standing in several inches of centuries-old black microbial ooze, which saturated their shoes and made the tunnel floor slippery.

They could go one of two directions, either ahead or behind where they were standing. They decided to start north, toward the palaces in which President Liu and President Ballinger had spent the night. As they walked, their breathing became labored and they were getting lightheaded, which Moretti suspected was from a lack of oxygen. He was about to suggest that they go back for a portable oxygen tank, when his light reflected off something metallic. Walking closer, he saw the metal steps of a rope ladder that ran to a circular hole in the roof of the tunnel. He had little doubt he'd find a throne room above.

Rather than ascend the ladder and leave, Moretti and Han Li decided to gut it out and try to find the tunnel's exit, to determine how the kidnappers had entered and escaped. Although they were already having difficulty breathing, they agreed that if things got bad, they could always return to this spot and exit the tunnel. In theory, that reasoning sounded good, but they were so driven to find the exit that they ignored their body's increased struggle for air.

It wasn't long before they reached a stone wall that blocked any further exploration. By that time they were gasping for air like guppies out of water, but they lacked the strength to retreat to the exit they'd found earlier. Moretti felt as if he had two competing super-migraines continually pulsating on either side of his head. He rested on a rock outcropping, trying to avoid sitting in the microbial ooze. Over and over again, he ran his flashlight over the surface of the stone wall blocking their path, failing to find a secret passage or doorway. They'd literally reached the end of their road, with no way forward or backward.

Han Li took a seat on a rock beside him and leaned back against the wall. Moretti guessed that her head felt the same as his, and that they were beginning to suffocate. They probably had no more than a few minutes before they'd lapse into unconsciousness. After that, they were as good as dead.

The lack of oxygen was beginning to affect his muscles, making his movements awkward and slightly spastic. As if on cue, his fingers involuntarily lost their grip on his flashlight, which dropped into the ooze at his feet. As he reached to pick it up, his hand brushed a long metal handle that was just below the surface. Not knowing or caring what it was, and with his lungs searing in pain, he pulled at the handle with all the strength he had left.

The handle moved six inches upward, followed by the sound of stone rubbing against stone. Moretti extended his hand down farther, grabbed his flashlight, and then pointed it at the wall blocking their path. It had moved away from him by several inches, partially revealing an opening. He and Han Li both stood, put their shoulders against the stone, and pushed with all their remaining strength. Inch by inch, the wall pivoted to the right and continued to open, until suddenly they felt an inflow of fresh air. At that moment, it felt to them like a shot of adrenaline.

Eventually, as the door continued to slowly open, they could see heavy foliage outside the tunnel. When they were finally able to make their way through the stone portal and out of the tunnel, Moretti and Han Li decided to go back and tell both security services what they'd discovered. This time, however, they'd take the surface route and enter the Forbidden City through the North Gate, which was directly across the street from them. As they crossed the service road, they found it odd that no security guards were around. They soon found out why—the gate was closed.

"That's just great," Moretti said. "You're a walking history book on this place. How far is it to the South Gate?"

"About a mile," said Han Li. "Then another three-quarters of a mile to traverse the Forbidden City to the palaces from which the presidents were kidnapped. That's where Agent Bonaquist and Yan He have their security offices."

"I hate to say it, but it'll take far less time if we go back into the tunnel and go up the rope ladder. Getting enough air shouldn't be a problem if we leave the tunnel door open."

Han Li agreed, so they reentered the tunnel and slogged their way through the fetid ooze until they found the rope ladder. When Moretti pushed back the throne chair, he immediately recognized the room from which President Ballinger had been abducted.

A Secret Service agent standing several feet away stumbled as he quickly distanced himself from the person who'd just poked his head through a large block of wood. The agent drew his gun, but fortunately refrained from shooting. Moretti stepped out of the hole, followed by Han Li, whose presence further surprised the agent. Both were handcuffed and lying facedown on the floor when Bonaquist arrived.

CHAPTER

5

After they were released from handcuffs, Moretti and Han Li told Bonaquist what they'd discovered. The veteran Secret Service agent had a difficult time accepting that his detail had missed the tunnel entrance that was directly under the throne in President Ballinger's quarters, but there was no arguing with the facts.

Bonaquist phoned the director of the US Secret Service in Washington and then Lieutenant Colonel Yan He, informing them of what he'd learned. His Chinese counterpart wasted no time in getting an experienced investigative crew into the tunnels. Heeding Moretti's advice, those who entered the tunnel first donned portable oxygen bottles and wore rubber boots. Fortunately those items had been stockpiled within the compound, along with other contingency supplies, for the gala.

Following his team's search of the tunnels, Yan He informed Bonaquist that they'd found dozens of entrances, each from underneath a throne chair in the numerous palaces scattered throughout the Inner Court of the Forbidden City. Yan He also confirmed that there was only one aboveground exit—the stone door Moretti and Han Li had discovered earlier across from the North Gate. In addition, his investigators had discovered numerous air vents in the ceiling of the tunnels, each of which emerged aboveground in innocuous locations. Most of the vents, however, had been destroyed over time and their inlets were clogged with debris. Therefore only a small amount of air, and some water, was able to get into the tunnel.

Yan He's men had also found supplies and equipment assumed to have been left behind by the kidnappers, including large oxygen tanks, breathing masks, backpacks, lanterns, batteries, empty food containers, and water bottles. This led him to conclude that they could have been underground for a full day.

"That's all very interesting, Lieutenant Colonel," said Bonaquist. "But I want to know how you plan to organize an effective search within Beijing, especially since Tianjin is only seventy-seven miles away." The head of the Secret Service detail knew that Beijing had a population of twenty-two million people, and Tianjin fifteen and a half million. He was certain that his superiors would be asking this very same question of him during their next phone call.

Yan He said, "Any vehicle attempting to leave Beijing or Tianjin will be thoroughly searched by the People's Liberation Army, which has more than enough manpower for this task. In addition, Acting President Ren Shi will broadcast an appeal to residents to call in anything they believe to be suspicious, and each report will be investigated by a two-man team. I'm about to send two hundred of my men to search every house and question every resident on the hill above the tunnel exit."

Bonaquist agreed that the lieutenant colonel's approach was all that could be done at that point. Trying to put a security perimeter around two cities with a combined population of more than thirty-seven million people sounded good in theory, but he doubted it would ensnare anyone who had been smart enough to abduct two presidents. "Is there anything the Secret Service can do to help?" he asked, in a somewhat mechanical response.

"Yes, let me get back to work." With that, Yan He terminated the call.

After concluding their debriefing with Bonaquist, Moretti and Han Li decided to return to their rooms and get cleaned up.

Halfway there, something caught Moretti's eye. He suddenly stopped and turned toward the hill that rose in the distance behind the North Gate. "Did you see that?" he asked.

"What?" Han Li replied, watching him step back about five feet. She didn't have a clue what he was talking about.

Moretti said, "Stand right here."

When Han Li did so, she saw light reflecting off what appeared to be a glass window at the top of the hill. "Do you mean the reflection?" she asked.

When Moretti nodded, Han Li continued, "There's bound to be houses up there. This is Beijing, where every sliver of land that's not government owned has something built on it."

"I understand. Let's put aside, for the moment, the question of how the kidnappers found out about the tunnels, of which apparently neither the People's Liberation Army nor the government officials involved with the gala were aware. Instead, let's focus on how you or I would go about this, if we had the same information possessed by the kidnappers."

"I'd position my men and equipment within the tunnels the day before, in the early morning hours when no one was around," Han Li said.

Moretti agreed. "Ditto. I'm betting that the kidnappers didn't drive their vehicles past the North Gate and right up to the tunnel entrance. There were too many security patrols around the Forbidden City when the presidents were in residence. So the kidnappers avoided detection by driving over that hill when everyone was asleep and continuing down to the stone outcropping."

"You think there's a way from one side of the hill to the other, and that they drove past the house at the top? Even if that roadway exists, what does that get us?"

"Possibly everything," Moretti said, without bothering to explain further.

Yan He had earlier ordered the North Gate opened so that

his men could easily access the tunnel exit. Moretti and Han Li took advantage of this. Showing the sentries the ID badges issued to them the previous day, they crossed the service road and found the dirt path leading up the hill.

"It's only a matter of time until we run into the lieutenant colonel," Han Li said. "He won't want us interfering with his investigation."

"Why not?" asked Moretti. "If it weren't for us, he'd still be scratching his head."

"He lost face because we discovered what his team had overlooked. He won't want to give us a second opportunity to make him look bad."

The road was becoming steeper, and as Moretti increased his stride, his back started to ache. Taking a deep breath, he continued to match Han Li's pace, but it wasn't easy. "If I'm correct," he said, "we're going to make Yan He look even worse."

"What does that mean?"

"I believe that part of the answer to the question of who kidnapped the presidents and government officials is up there," he said, pointing in front of him. "And I think I know exactly where to look."

Han Li wanted a further explanation, but Moretti said he'd explain when they got to the summit. On their ascent, they passed a raft of Chinese military who were apparently conducting door-to-door searches and questioning residents. Moretti and Han Li were stopped twice and asked for their identifications. In both instances, they presented their Forbidden City passes and were allowed to continue. A hundred yards below the crest of the hill, however, they ran into the lieutenant colonel.

"Why are you here?" Yan He asked, clearly surprised to see them. "This is a military investigation zone. Only my men, along with the residents, are allowed on this hill."

"We're all on the same team, sir. In fact, we're the ones who found the tunnel entrance," Moretti replied.

"Yes, but you reported it to Agent Bonaquist instead of to me. Just so there's no future misunderstanding, I'm in charge of security on Chinese soil—not your American Secret Service. Leave this area immediately. If you don't, I'll have you both arrested." And with that, Yan He turned and walked away.

"So much for gratitude," said Moretti.

Han Li replied, "We made him look bad."

"If I'm right, he's soon going to be at the bottom of a very steep hill with an ocean of sewage coming his way. Given what happened, why hasn't he been fired? That would seem to be a foregone conclusion with a security failure of this magnitude."

"I don't know, but it does seem strange. Are we going back to the Forbidden City?" Han Li asked.

"Not a chance. If Yan He wants to arrest me, he'll have to come and get me," Moretti said as he continued walking.

At the crest of the hill was a home surrounded by a ten-foot redbrick wall, which itself was largely hidden behind dense shrubbery. And just as Moretti had anticipated, the dirt path continued past the house and over the crest of the hill. Han Li watched as Moretti began pulling aside the shrubbery at various intervals, apparently looking for something. Five minutes later he stepped out of the dense foliage.

Walking to the two steel gates that guarded the entrance to the residence, he pressed the red button on the intercom box. "I think I found something," he said to Han Li, who was standing to his right. "Please ask whoever answers if we can come inside and speak with them."

"And if they ask me what this is about?"

"Think of something," Moretti answered.

Before she could respond, a metallic Chinese voice emanated from the speaker. A discussion soon ensued, and before long the gates began to open.

"What did he say?" Moretti asked.

"He asked what we want," said Han Li. "I told him that we

work for the government and that we'd like to speak with him. He didn't sound happy, and he told me he'd just been questioned by an army colonel. But eventually he agreed to cooperate."

The gates opened to reveal a flagstone-covered courtyard, in the center of which was an ornate fountain with two leaping dolphins spewing water toward each other. The man walking toward them appeared to be in his early sixties. He was five foot seven, thin, and dressed in a dark blue golf shirt and crisply pressed tan slacks.

Han Li showed him the identification card attached to the lanyard around her neck, and she and Moretti were led to the front door of the house. As they walked, the man pressed the remote-control device in his hand, and the gates silently closed behind them.

Outside the front door he removed his shoes and changed into a pair of sandals. He handed Moretti and Han Li each a pair of sandals, and seeing that their socks were coated in the same black sediment as their shoes, asked them to remove their socks as well. When they had complied and donned their plastic footwear, they all went inside.

The interior of the house was significantly different from what Moretti had expected. It was furnished, not in an Oriental motif, but in a Western minimalist style done in grays, black, and white. Bright white ceramic tiles covered the floors throughout, and a huge picture window provided natural light that enlivened the interior. The only splash of color came from two red chairs in the living room, which were a stunning contrast to the gray walls they rested against.

The man directed them to a black couch and sat in one of the red chairs across from them. Han Li began conversing with him in Chinese, after which she interpreted for Moretti.

"He says Yan He questioned him for about twenty minutes while soldiers searched his property, and then they all left. He's asking me if he's being questioned a second time because he's a suspect. I told him not as far as I know, but that we represent a government agency and not the military."

"Did the lieutenant colonel ask if this home has a surveillance system?"

Han Li asked, and the man responded that Yan He hadn't.

"Then please ask if we can look at the recordings from last night," said Moretti.

The expression on Han Li's face reflected that she now understood why Moretti had immersed himself in the shrubbery. He had been trying to see if the house was equipped with surveillance cameras. She asked the question and received an immediate response.

"He says that he does, and he'll show them to us," she said. The man got up and led them to a small room to the left of the entryway.

Like the rest of the house, it was sparsely furnished. Against the far wall was a white lacquer desk, in the center of which was a twenty-seven-inch, all-in-one computer and screen. In front of the computer sat a keyboard and, to the right of that, what looked to be a video recorder. A single white chair was in front of the desk.

Moretti said, "Ask him if we can see the recording from the security camera facing the dirt path leading to his residence."

As Han Li interpreted, the man turned on the computer and hit a few keys. The screen split into a dozen images of his property, and he brought up the requested view.

"That's it," Moretti said.

Han Li spoke to the man, who showed her several functions on the keyboard and then departed.

"Where he'd go?" asked Moretti.

"I asked if he'd show me how to use the system and then give us some privacy."

"Good call. Let's see what we've got."

Han Li typed "2:00 a.m." in the time display box in the lower right corner of her screen and then clicked Play. At a thirty-frame-per-second recording speed, the resolution was excellent, even in night vision mode. For the next thirty-six minutes, the monitor displayed only the darkness of night.

But a minute later two panel vans came into view, passed the residence as they descended the hill, and stopped directly across from the dense growth that hid the tunnel exit. Han Li zoomed in and they both watched as seconds later, the tunnel door inched open and the hostages, whose movements appeared uncoordinated and sluggish, were dragged out of the tunnel. The kidnapper's faces were hidden by balaclavas, but all were of average build and height—except for one who looked as if he belonged on the offensive line of an NFL team. When everyone was inside the vans, the drivers retraced their route, passing the residence and continuing over the crest of the hill.

"I didn't see a license plate or any identifying marks on the vans," Moretti said.

Han Li agreed. "Nor did I."

"Any suggestions on how we can find out where they went?" asked Moretti. "Right now, I'm drawing a blank."

"There may be a way."

Moretti had expected Han Li to agree that they had no chance of tracking the vans, so he was surprised at her response. "Do you really think you can find these vehicles?"

"Possibly," she said.

"How?"

"Follow me." Han Li didn't explain. Instead, she ejected the DVD and put it in her jacket pocket, then left the room. Moretti scrambled after her. They thanked the owner of the house for his cooperation and then left the residence.

Han Li led the way, this time following the dirt road over the crest of the hill, the same route the two vans had taken on the previous night. A half mile from the house, they came to a highway. Except for the occasional taxi, Beijing's normally clogged streets seemed to be unusually empty. Moretti thought that most people must be inside watching the news, since word of the abductions had almost certainly been released.

Han Li held up her arm and, several minutes later, signaled a passing taxi. Once inside, she told the driver where she wanted to go, and then she hit a speed-dial number on her cell phone. The ensuing conversation lasted five minutes.

When she finished, she shifted in her seat and faced Moretti. "We're going to see a friend of my late uncle."

"What does your uncle's friend do?" asked Moretti.

"Yangfeng Hao runs our country's domestic surveillance and camera monitoring network."

Then Moretti understood how they might be able to track the vehicles. China was widely considered to have one of the largest domestic surveillance systems in the world. From what he'd heard, that network was especially pervasive in Beijing, the Chinese equivalent of Washington, DC.

Their taxi soon stopped in front of a large, nondescript office building whose bland appearance told Moretti that it probably belonged to the government. Military troops were thick in the area, and three soldiers surrounded the cab when it pulled to the curb. Moretti and Han Li showed the IDs that they had been issued the previous day, but that apparently didn't carry much weight. They were ordered to immediately get back into the taxi and leave, even after Han Li told the soldiers that they were there to meet Yangfeng Hao.

Just sixteen weeks earlier, the three young men had been working on a farm. Now they understood only the singular order given to them by their commander: no one without a building identification card gets past them. As Han Li continued to protest, one of the three ran out of patience with what he apparently perceived to be civil disobedience. Grabbing her with one arm and Moretti with the other, he pulled them toward a military van.

Halfway to the van, a heavyset man in his early sixties walked up to the soldier. Bald except for half a dozen strands of dyed black hair arranged in a comb-over, the man wore tan slacks and a faded red golf shirt. He showed his ID and apparently exerted his authority, based on the tone of the conversation. The young soldier released Moretti and Han Li, saluted the man, and rejoined his two comrades.

Yangfeng Hao gave Han Li a long embrace, and after a few minutes of what sounded to Moretti like chitchat, he handed them their building passes. Then he led them through the military perimeter surrounding the building and into the lobby of the thirty-story tower. After passing through security, they took the elevator to the twelfth floor and followed Hao to a corner office.

In deference to Moretti, Han Li began speaking to Hao in English, a language in which he was apparently fluent. She asked if he could track two white vans for her. Without waiting for a response, she then removed the DVD from her jacket pocket and handed it to him. Hao didn't ask why she needed the information. Instead, he inserted the disk into his computer and clicked an icon on the screen. Han Li asked him to fast-forward to 2:37 a.m.

As he watched his computer screen, Hao became visibly shaken. "Have you shown this to anyone?" he asked, taking a handkerchief from his back pocket and wiping his brow.

"Not yet," Han Li replied.

"If it was anyone other than you, I'd say immediately give this disk to the government and keep a low profile. But that's not you. I know what you're capable of, and I can only assume the company you keep has similar qualifications. I'll help you any way I can."

"Thank you," said Han Li.

"Let's see where these vans went," Hao continued. "Can you tell me where this surveillance video was taken?"

Han Li gave him the location of the residence. Then Hao took a deep breath and began typing commands into his computer. Eventually he found a surveillance camera that was near the intersection of the dirt road and the highway. Accessing its digital record, he went to 2:37 a.m. Three minutes later the vans appeared and Hao began tracking their progress, transitioning from one surveillance camera to another as the vans headed east across the city. Eventually they entered the mountains to the north, the termination point for the Beijing surveillance network.

Hao said a curse word in Chinese. "They've just entered an area where we have no monitoring system."

"You don't have any cameras on the mountain pass road?" Han Li asked.

"We have four hundred thousand surveillance cameras in Beijing. That network doesn't extend into the mountains, but don't worry. I can access Tianjin's system and pick the vans up there."

"Tianjin?" Moretti asked, as Hao began furiously typing on his keyboard.

Han Li explained, "A city of twelve million people on the other side of the mountains. I've driven the pass road many times, and there are no turnoffs before they enter Tianjin."

When Hao's cell phone rang, he put it in the crook of his neck as he continued to type commands into his computer terminal. As Moretti and Han Li watched the elderly government official, they saw a flash of surprise materialize on his face. Hao immediately left the surveillance program, opened an internet browser, and began typing a string of numbers and letters that were apparently being given to him by the caller. When he finished, he hit the Enter key and a video appeared.

Both presidents, along with the four abducted Chinese officials, were wearing orange jumpsuits and kneeling next to one another. In back and to the right of them was a large rectangular black flag, with crossed gold scimitars at the top and Arabic writing below it.

"Islamic terrorists?" Han Li asked in wonderment.

"Of the worst type," Moretti answered. "I recognize their

flag. They're an Islamic extremist group known as the Protectors of Islam. I had a few run-ins with them in Afghanistan. They mercilessly murder anyone who ideologically opposes them, including their own families. Their mantra is that all foreigners must leave the Middle East. Anyone who doesn't leave is automatically sentenced to death—and therefore considered fair game for their followers."

Hao paused the video to more clearly hear what Moretti was saying.

"The Protectors, as most refer to them, also believe that Islamic law, or *sharia*, was prescribed by Allah and therefore must be enforced globally. Under sharia, religion and government become one, human rights are rejected, and democracy is nonexistent. The Protectors' founder is Awalmir Afridi, a radical Dawari from the Karlani Pashtun tribe. The last I heard, he was believed to be hiding in the tribal area of Pakistan. His followers, believed to number more than two hundred thousand, are spread throughout the Middle East and Africa. Afridi is nicknamed 'the butcher' because of the horrific way he publicly executes his enemies and then posts their deaths on the internet."

When Moretti finished his explanation, Hao resumed the video. Behind each hostage stood a man wearing a black balaclava and sunglasses, holding a knife to the throat of the person kneeling before him. A whiteboard was rolled in front of the camera, listing the kidnappers' demands in both Chinese and English. The first was that China pay a ransom of $5 billion in gold. The second mandated that the United States and its allies withdraw their troops and advisers from the Middle East within three days—by 6:00 p.m. Beijing time—and leave behind all military arms and equipment. If those demands were met, the presidents would be released unharmed. If not, all captives would be beheaded. An internet address appeared at the bottom of the whiteboard.

Moretti wondered why they didn't mention releasing the other prisoners and why they used a whiteboard instead of audibly giving their terms. He was thinking about that when Hao, who fortunately had the presence of mind to copy down the internet address written on the whiteboard, typed it on his keyboard and hit the Enter key. Another video immediately appeared.

The second video showed Tang Ji, minister of national defense, in the same room but kneeling by himself. Behind him was the huge person whom Moretti and Han Li had seen coming out of the tunnel exit. He was wearing a balaclava and holding a knife to the throat of the blindfolded government official.

Moretti thought that Tang appeared to be much too calm for someone who was blindfolded and kneeling with a steel blade pressed against his neck. The only reasonable explanation he could come up with was that the minister was drugged and therefore largely unaware of what was happening.

The camera zoomed in until Tang's head and shoulders took up the entire field of vision. Moretti knew what would come next, but before he could warn the others, the minister's hair was roughly pulled back and the blade sliced across his neck. Four strokes were required to complete the decapitation, during which the arterial spray engulfed the killer as well as his victim.

Hao became violently ill and grabbed his wastepaper basket, throwing up whatever he had inside him. More accustomed to seeing the darker side of life, Moretti and Han Li continued watching the video. Both appeared emotionless, but Moretti knew that was just a façade. Long ago he had learned that internalizing his anger helped him to effectively focus his wrath. He assumed that Han Li had come to the same conclusion, since she didn't say a word.

One way or another, Moretti was going to send the coward standing behind his decapitated victim to either Allah or hell—his choice.

CHAPTER

6

North Waziristan is a mountainous region in northwest Pakistan that borders Afghanistan. The area is littered with deep, rugged passes and gorges that form a rampart between the two countries. The region has slightly fewer than 400,000 inhabitants, so outsiders are easily recognized and encouraged to leave.

In a small, innocuous brick dwelling at the edge of the mountain village of Razmak, Awalmir Afridi sat cross-legged on the floor and watched a recording of Tang Ji's beheading. The founder of the Protectors of Islam was five foot eight and a muscular 150 pounds, and had a rock-solid physique maintained by a daily three-hour regimen of exercise. His unruly black beard did little to soften the hard-bitten expression permanently etched on his hatchet face, and he was bald except for a broad pasting of hair above each ear.

Afridi didn't have internet access or a cellular phone, because he knew either of those would eventually lead the Americans to him. Then it wouldn't be long before a drone strike relieved him of all earthly concerns. He was looking at a video, made by one of his followers with his movie camera, that he brought up on his computer screen.

Afridi had overcome many obstacles to establish and grow the Protectors of Islam. In the early days he had struggled, barely able to raise enough money from supporters to feed his small band of followers. It wasn't until later, when a Dubai filmmaker produced a documentary on his group, that he had gained notoriety. After that, money from Iran and Saudi Arabia, as well as other sponsors of terrorism, had flowed to him. With his newly found fame and wealth, Afridi had been able to attract tens of thousands of followers, purchase a vast quantity of weapons, and bribe officials to ignore his activities.

He had chosen the name of his group as a public statement that Afridi was the chief defender of his religion. He advocated that Islamic law, or sharia, in which religious and government dictates are looked upon as being one and the same, had been prescribed by Allah and therefore must be enforced globally. Therefore his stated goal was to kill or drive away every foreigner in the Middle East and Africa to protect the cultural and religious integrity of both regions.

Privately, Afridi couldn't have cared less about an influx of foreigners. His real agenda was to rid those areas of outside influence so that he could effectively control the nations within them and exploit their wealth. In countries where his followers had a foothold, government officials paid handsomely for Afridi's pledge not to fuel secular unrest. If anyone failed to make an agreed-upon payment or challenged his leadership dictums, he dealt with the offenders harshly. Usually that involved killing the person who had failed to live up to their agreement or inciting riots until that person was overthrown. When word of these actions got around, most payments to his organization arrived early—and none were late.

This influence made Afridi the undisputed leader of his group, and no important decision was made without his explicit approval. That's why it came as a shock when some of his followers apparently took it upon themselves to kidnap two of the most powerful heads of state in the world, along with several high-ranking Chinese officials, and then even behead one hostage. Afridi didn't know who had planned or organized the abductions, or where they got the financial resources and necessary intelligence to carry out such an audacious operation in a country where they had only a microscopic presence. But it was critical that he find that person before they became a hero to his followers and, more importantly, his sponsors.

The problem was that he didn't have an inkling whom it might be. In his opinion, none of his followers were even remotely smart enough to have planned and executed the kidnappings—and yet it had happened. The flag of the Protectors of Islam, which could be seen behind the hostages in the video, proved that. Obviously the mastermind behind this operation didn't want to reveal himself too soon, probably fearing that the leadership of the Protectors would either take credit for the operation and marginalize his contribution—or kill him. He voted for the latter.

He could hear gunfire erupting throughout the village as his people celebrated Allah's great triumph, but that would soon change. Afridi needed to expose and kill this madman because a sword has two sides. If anything happened to the president of the United States, as he believed it would, the largest military in the world was going to take retribution against his group, which permeated virtually every country in the Middle East and most of Africa.

Today Afridi was joyfully celebrated by his followers for accomplishing the impossible. But when the Americans unleashed their fury upon those same followers—their loved ones killed and their homes reduced to rubble—this admiration would turn to scorn. Even if Afridi somehow survived, he'd become the new Osama bin Laden. Everyone knew how that had turned out—killed while resisting capture, a burial at sea, and a smudged footnote in the annals of history. Afridi was in a serious bind, and the only chance he had to survive and maintain the status quo was to find the person responsible for the abductions.

Ren Shi was five foot eight inches tall, with a thick torso that made him look more like a nightclub bouncer than a senior government official. His black hair, dyed so that not a fleck of gray could be found, was short and brushed straight back. He was a career politician, known by those who mattered to have reached his equilibrium of competence. As a result, the Party had designated his replacement, someone who they believed had the wherewithal to one day assume the country's leadership. He'd be expected to show his successor the ropes and ease him into the number three position in the government. If he cooperated, he'd receive a generous retirement allowance, along with a home and domestic staff for the rest of his life. If he didn't, he'd be maligned, accused of corruption, and left to fend for himself. Not much of a choice.

However, early this morning, with the announcement that President Liu and Senior Vice Premier Chen Gaoli had been abducted, Ren Shi's world had changed. The second vice premier became the acting leader of China, making him one of the most important people in the world. He'd never had so much power, and the thought of dispensing it made him euphoric. Next week, if all went as planned, he'd become the permanent president of his country—and put $2.5 billion in his pocket.

Once the color had returned to Yangfeng Hao's face, he went back to his keyboard and continued his efforts to try to find the vans. For the next three hours, along with Han Li and Moretti, he looked carefully at every vehicle exiting the Tianjin side of the mountain pass. But none of the three sets of eyes glued to the screen could find the vehicles. Neither did they see, when Hao reaccessed the last camera on the Beijing side of the pass, the vans return to the city.

"Where could they be?" Hao asked.

"The only possible explanation is that they're in the mountains between the two cities. They couldn't just disappear," Moretti said.

"I surveyed the entire region ten years ago, when this system was first being installed," Hao said. "At that time, the brush was so dense that it'd take heavy construction equipment to go even a moderate distance off the main highway. When I drove the road last year, I saw that nothing had changed. It's all but impossible to drive or even walk more than fifty feet from the highway. A more likely explanation for the disappearance of the vans is that the kidnappers knew the limits of our surveillance system, had alternate vehicles waiting for them in the pass, and transferred their captives to them. I have to believe that if we search hard enough, we'll find the vans hidden in the brush."

Moretti agreed with Hao. Given that the vehicles hadn't evaporated into thin air, they had to still be in the pass. He and Han Li left Hao's office and handed their visitor badges to the security officer as they left the building.

"I'd like to drive through that mountain pass and have a look for myself. Any idea where we can rent a car?" Moretti asked as they walked toward the highway to summon a taxi.

"Before we do that," said Han Li, "we need to see Gao Hui."

"The old guy who helped us out this morning?"

Han Li corrected him. "A respected elder on the Politburo Standing Committee. We need him to protect us from Yan He. As soon as the lieutenant colonel finds out what we've been up to, he'll have us arrested."

"I tend to agree with you," said Moretti, "since he told us as much when we saw him earlier today. I don't want to find out what the inside of a People's Liberation Army prison looks like, so why don't you give him a call?"

There was no traffic as their taxi sped the mile and a half to where Gao worked. As they pulled up in front of a complex of rectangular, multistory office buildings, Han Li pointed to the building that housed the Politburo Standing Committee.

"Looks like we have another reception committee," Moretti said as he looked out the window of the taxi.

It didn't take more than a few seconds, after their vehicle

stopped, for one of the four-man security patrols to approach and surround their taxi. As he and Han Li got out of the backseat, Moretti fully expected to be manhandled by the soldiers, who were wearing combat gear, and then questioned by the approaching officer. Instead, none of the four men moved until the officer arrived. The army major asked their names and, upon confirmation that he was speaking to the individuals he'd been told to expect, dismissed his men. He introduced himself and said they were expected, thanks to Han Li's call, and that he'd escort them through the remaining layers of security and up to Gao's office.

They got off at the thirtieth floor, where the major used his security card to open a door to the right of the elevator. They walked down a dimly lit corridor, with thick red carpet and deep cherrywood paneling, that dead-ended at a closed door. Knocking twice before entering, the major led them into the office of Gao's executive assistant. Then he excused himself and left.

The slender five-foot-four woman, who appeared to be in her mid-fifties, had short black hair, prominent cheekbones, a small nose, and an ingratiating smile. She wore a black skirt and white blouse with no jewelry. She silently led Moretti and Han Li through a door directly behind her desk. The room they entered, approximately thirty feet square, was adorned with thick Oriental carpets laid over antique, wide-plank oak flooring. At the back of the room was a hand-carved oak desk and a matching straight-back chair.

Gao, upon seeing them, stood from his desk and came toward them. "It's good to see you both again," he said, shaking Moretti's hand and giving Han Li an affectionate hug. "Please sit down." He pointed to four yoke-back chairs surrounding a small circular conference table, which was to their right.

"You indicated you had something important that you wanted to share with me," continued Gao when everyone was seated.

"This is a video recording of the kidnapping," said Han Li,

taking the DVD from the pocket of her leather jacket and handing it to him.

Gao seemed to be taken aback and slowly reached for the disk. Going back to his desk, he watched the video on his computer. "How did you come by this?" he asked, returning to the conference table.

Han Li explained how they'd obtained it. Then she told him about Yan He's warning that they cease their investigation of the abductions.

Gao asked, "Who else has seen this?"

Han Li told him that Yangfeng Hao was the only other person who'd seen it, and that he'd helped them track the vans to the mountain pass at the southeastern edge of the city where video surveillance ended. At that point, she explained, the vans seemed to have disappeared since they never entered Tianjin.

"They switched vehicles?" asked Gao.

Han Li replied, "That's what we're thinking."

"Don't concern yourselves with Yan He. I'll speak to him." Then, changing the subject, Gao asked, "Have you seen the beheading of Minister Tang Ji?"

They acknowledged that they had.

"We can't allow the same fate to befall the presidents," said Gao, "or the remaining hostages. Despite using our vast and intricate arrays of human and electronic intelligence resources in conducting this search, our governments are getting nowhere. That's because China and the United States are both hopelessly mired in bureaucracy, and neither country is therefore capable of succeeding within such a short time frame. But the two of you don't suffer from that same affliction."

Suddenly an idea seemed to come to Gao. He walked to the door, opened it, and said something to his assistant. Not long afterward, she escorted a photographer, carrying a camera and a retractable white screen, into the office. "I'm going to issue you both government credentials," Gao said. The photographer took their photographs and left. Fifteen minutes later, Gao's assistant returned and handed him two laminated ID cards.

"This is a Politburo Standing Committee staff ID card for you, Miss Li," Gao said, handing it to her. "And Mr. Moretti, this is a PSC foreigner pass for you. Since you now technically work for this committee, these ID cards will allow you to conduct your search without hindrance. Since you arrived by taxi, it appears that you also need a car. Please take mine." Removing a key from his pocket, Gao handed it to Han Li and told her where his car was parked. "My license plate identifies the driver as a senior government official, which means you probably won't be stopped at any of the security checkpoints now in place within the city."

Gao stood, indicating that their meeting was over. "I should mention that this morning, because of the heightened state of alert for government officials, the military borrowed my car key to place what they described as 'protective gear' in the trunk of my vehicle," he said, escorting them to the door. "You might want to check it out."

Moretti and Han Li thanked Gao for his assistance and took the elevator down to the parking garage. There they found the black Audi A5 in a nearby cordoned-off area.

"Before we get going, let's have a look at the protective gear," Moretti said as he took the key from Han Li and pressed the trunk release on the key fob.

Apparently the military's definition of protective gear was quite broad. They found two Norinco Type 92 semi-automatic handguns, a QBB-95 SAW rifle, numerous boxes of spare ammunition, and equipment that seemed well suited for use by a Special Forces unit. Moretti speculated that the gear was meant for Gao's security detail.

With their newly issued ID cards, a car, and enough armament to win most firefights, Moretti and Han Li decided that the first thing they needed to do was get a detailed look at the mountain pass. The drive went smoothly and, with their government license plate, the Audi was given expedited passage through every checkpoint.

They entered the mountains southeast of the city an hour after they left Gao's office and drove straight through to Tianjin. Along the way they saw no sign of the vans nor any highways or local roads branching off the two-lane strip of asphalt that wound through the pass. The brush and vegetation were just as Yangfeng Hao had described—far too thick for a van, or any vehicle, for that matter—to penetrate.

"We missed something," Moretti said, the disappointment obvious in his voice as he entered Tianjin and took the first exit off the main highway. "Since the surveillance cameras didn't show the vans exiting either end of the pass, obviously they must still be there—somewhere." He pulled the car onto a side street and turned off the engine.

"I agree," said Han Li. "Turn around and let's take another look."

"Before we do that, let's put ourselves in the mind-set of the kidnappers. They've just abducted two of the most important people on the planet, along with four senior Chinese government officials. They're not sure whether one or both security details will check on their president during the night or leave him undisturbed until morning, which is what happened. Therefore, to them, time is of the essence. So I don't believe they'd drive all the way to Tianjin. Instead …"

"They'd switch vehicles and return to Beijing—and their secure hiding place," Han Li said, finishing Moretti's thought.

"The kidnappers have demonstrated that they're meticulous planners," said Moretti. "Therefore it's safe to assume that they're sufficiently familiar with the Beijing surveillance system to know its boundaries."

"And that's why they drove into the pass, so they could switch vehicles undetected."

"Exactly. Also, since time is critical, the vehicle transfer probably happened only a short distance beyond the last surveillance camera."

Han Li asked, "You think the vans are hidden at the Beijing end of the pass?"

"I do. And finding them is critical because right now we have nothing else to go on. Those vans are the only lead we have," said Moretti.

As they drove back to Beijing, Han Li called Yangfeng Hao and got the geographic coordinates of the last surveillance camera, which she put into her cell phone. Meanwhile Moretti had the pedal to the metal. The Audi flew through the mountain pass and arrived at the GPS location indicated on Han Li's cell phone in just forty-five minutes. Then Moretti made a U-turn and proceeded back toward Tianjin, this time at a much slower speed.

Four minutes later, out of the corner of his eye, he saw a glint of sun reflecting off metal. Slamming on the brakes, he brought the Audi to a screeching halt. To their left, thirty yards from the main highway, was a three-by-four-foot rectangular metal sign nearly obscured by brush, with black Chinese characters on it. According to Han Li, who could translate only what she could see, it read "IWHR."

Now that the car was stopped, they could also see, to the left of the sign, a six-foot-wide road that squeezed through the brush and vegetation and led inland. The turnoff to this road was at the beginning of a hairpin turn in the highway, which meant that the focus of any driver would be directly in front of them. If someone didn't know where the narrow road was, he or she would probably miss it.

Moretti eased the Audi off the highway and started inland. As they drove, Han Li explained that IWHR was the public utility that provided Beijing with water, electric power, hydropower, and sewage treatment. Only half listening, Moretti swiveled his head from side to side as he drove between the dense brush, thinking that this area would be the perfect spot for an ambush.

Three hundred yards from the highway, the narrow road ended at an area surrounded by an eight-foot-high chain-link fence, with a sliding roll-gate as its single point of entry. Connecting to either side of the gate, the fence, which was covered in vegetative growth, extended in both directions as far as the eye could see. "We know someone's been here," said Moretti. "The gate, and where it connects to the fence, is clean of vegetation."

"And the road, such as it was, is also relatively clear," Han Li added.

They got out of the car, approached the gate, and saw that a lock secured it to the metal frame bordering the fence.

"This is a hidden shackle lock, generally considered unpickable," Han Li said. "It's unusual to see a utility company using such an expensive lock."

"Can you pick it?"

"Maybe, but it will take quite some time," she said, removing a leather pouch from her jacket pocket.

"Wait, I think I can speed up the process," Moretti said, opening the trunk of their car and removing a rifle. "You might want to step away. It's been a while since I was on the practice range." He loaded a round in the chamber and aimed the crosshairs of the scope at the circular target, which resembled a hockey puck. A moment later there was a sharp crack and the lock jerked.

Han Li examined the hole directly into its center and saw that the lock had released. She threw the broken pieces of the locking device to the ground and rolled open the gate. "Wouldn't a handgun have been easier?" she asked, walking back to the car.

"Handguns don't have the penetrating power of a rifle," Moretti said, putting the rifle back in the trunk. "In Afghanistan, I fired a .357 bullet into a similar lock, and it still held tight. One of the guys in my unit then pumped a round from his rifle into it and the lock flew apart. A handgun works perfectly only in the movies."

"Good to know," said Han Li.

They got back into the car and drove past the open gate. The brush and vegetation were still thick and high on either side of them, and the path remained narrow as their vehicle crept forward at ten miles per hour. Suddenly, a quarter mile later, as they went over a rise in the road, they found themselves in a clearing. Before them was a huge reservoir extending far into the distance. To their right stood two metal sheds, each half a football field long and thirty yards wide, with pitched aluminum roofs that rose to a height of nearly twenty feet.

Moretti stopped the car, turned off the ignition, and popped the trunk. He removed two handguns and flashlights, handing one of each to Han Li. "We don't know what we'll run into. Better to be prepared," he said, racking the slide on his Norinco Type 92 semi-automatic. Han Li did the same. "Let's start here," Moretti said, pointing to the shed closest to them.

The door was locked, but without a dead bolt, blocking plate, or protective molding, it might as well have been left open. Han Li was able to slide a credit card into the vertical crack between the door and doorjamb and throw it open with ease. The interior was pitch black. Moretti used his flashlight to scour the interior walls next to the door until he found the master light control panel. As he pushed the throw switch upward, he heard a series of clicks. Large mercury vapor lamps, in two rows across the ceiling, gradually came to life and bathed the interior in light.

Exposed before them was a series of huge pumps, arranged linearly from one end of the shed to the other, moving vast quantities of water from the reservoir to the city of Beijing. Moretti and Han Li searched the entire building, but they failed to turn up any evidence that the vans, kidnappers, or hostages had ever been there.

The second building was also locked, and Han Li again took out her credit card and easily opened the door. Once the mercury vapor lamps came to full power, they saw that this shed seemed to be the utility's maintenance facility. Directly in front of them were heavy steel racks extending from floor to ceiling and containing pipes of various lengths, diameters, and curvatures. Next was a long row of gray metal shelves stocked with electrical motors and various other supplies. However, as they gradually searched the building, Moretti and Han Li found that the racks of pipes and supplies occupied only the front half of the shed.

The rear of the facility was empty—except for two white vans parked in front of a pull-chain doorway. Moretti felt an adrenaline rush. At that moment, he had no doubt that they'd found what they were looking for. But as he got closer to the vehicles, he wasn't quite so sure. Both vans had license plates and the utility company's logo prominently displayed on their exteriors.

Curious, he ran his hand over the company's name on one van, expecting it to be vinyl film that could easily be attached and removed. Instead, he found that the logo was painted on. He was about to start his search of the vehicle's interior when he felt something sticky on his hand. Scraping at it with his fingernail, he saw that he had picked up some sort of adhesive from the logo.

"Look here," Han Li shouted, interrupting his train of thought.

When Moretti turned around, he saw that she was standing next to a trash bin and holding two large sheets of white plastic film. "They covered the logos by gluing these sheets over them," said Han Li.

"That makes sense, since I found adhesive on the side panel of this van. Let's see what we find inside," Moretti said. He walked to the back of the vehicle, followed by Han Li. Opening the rear cargo doors, he was not surprised to find the interior as empty and pristine as the day it came off the assembly line.

As he climbed inside the van, Moretti detected a sweet odor that increased in intensity as he moved to the front of the vehicle. The smell seemed familiar, but he had difficulty placing it. Eventually he found a white cotton rag under the passenger seat. Putting the rag to his nose to see if it was the source of the odor, he immediately became dizzy. Then he recalled his first encounter with that same sweet scent—in the remote villages of Afghanistan where doctors still used trichloromethane, commonly known as chloroform, to sedate patients.

Moretti dropped the rag and exited the van, needing to get some fresh air and clear his head. As he did so, he saw Han Li exit the other van while holding a pair of flex cuffs.

"I found these under the driver's seat," she said, handing them to Moretti. "Not exactly standard issue for utilities."

He said, "It looks like these are our vehicles. Now where the hell are the hostages?"

When they returned to the Forbidden City, they were told that their luggage had been taken to the St. Regis Hotel. Moretti was thankful for the move, which meant that he could now shower, shave, and change clothes. Traffic was light, so it took only fifteen minutes to get to the hotel. Most people had elected to stay home from work and remain glued to their TVs for any news updates.

Upon entering the hotel lobby, Moretti and Han Li attracted the attention of everyone within eyeshot. Their clothes—wrinkled, dirty, and still damp from trudging through the tunnel early that morning—were in sharp contrast to the hotel's business casual atmosphere. When they got to the front desk, which was on the left side of the lobby, they registered and were given keys to rooms on the second floor. The clerk said their bags had been taken upstairs earlier that day, so they started toward the elevator. But then the smell of food from the dining room, which was diagonally across from the registration desk, caught their attention. Since it had been almost twenty-four hours since they'd eaten, they decided to go straight to the hotel's restaurant before going upstairs.

They entered the dining room during the dinner rush, so there wasn't an empty table in sight. Because of their appearance, the hostess asked to see their room keys before taking their names.

Since it would be at least an hour before they could be seated, she recommended, as an alternative, that they order room service. Just as Moretti and Han Li were about to take her suggestion, they heard someone calling their names. Looking up, they saw Bonaquist in the distance, sitting at a table by himself.

He waved them over and asked, "Why don't you both join me?"

They readily accepted his offer, and the waitress handed them menus. Wasting no time, Moretti ordered a rib-eye steak and baked potato, along with a cup of coffee. Han Li had grilled salmon, some sort of vegetable with which neither Moretti nor Bonaquist was familiar, and hot green tea. When the waitress left, Moretti and Han Li excused themselves and went to the restrooms to clean up as best they could.

When they returned, they found the Secret Service agent rubbing his forehead. "I don't mind telling you that every politician and a fair chunk of the American people want me roasted on a spit," he told them without preamble. "If it hadn't been for what you two discovered this morning, the politicians would have probably sacrificed me. As it is, since even President Liu's security detail didn't know about the tunnel, your discovery made it seem as if we were the more professional of the two organizations that lost a sitting president."

"It wasn't your fault," said Moretti.

"Whatever goes wrong when guarding the president of the United States is, by definition, my fault. I never thought about putting the GPR over the throne, but I obviously should have."

"Spilled milk," Moretti replied. "This'll cheer you up. We have a video of the kidnapping, and we found the kidnappers' vans."

Suddenly alert, Bonaquist sat up in his chair and asked, "How? Where?"

"The *where* is a municipal utility shed adjacent to the reservoir north of the city," explained Moretti. "But don't get too excited, because you won't find much there. The *how* led us there." He went on to detail their day, beginning with the video they had retrieved from the home at the top of the hill, their visits to Yangfeng Hao and Gao Hui, and finally what they had found inside the vans.

"I need a copy of the kidnapping video as soon as possible," insisted Bonaquist.

"I'll text Gao and ask him to send it to you," Han Li said, taking her cell phone out of her jacket pocket.

"Great detective work," said Bonaquist. "I mean it. You two seem to have your fingers on the pulse of what's happening, while the rest of us are wandering around like lemmings." After getting precise directions to the reservoir from Han Li, he took a cell phone from his pants pocket, called another agent, and repeated the directions to that agent. Ending the call, he told Han Li and Moretti, "I'll give Yan He this information. He's going to really love you two for upstaging him a second time."

"If you could," Han Li requested, "please don't mention our visit to Yangfeng Hao. I don't want to get him in trouble."

"I don't remember a Yangfeng Hao," said Bonaquist. "Must be early-stage Alzheimer's. I'll let Yan He guess how you two found the vans. That should drive him nuts."

Moretti laughed, and Han Li thanked Bonaquist.

"But I do have a question for you, Ms. Li," added Bonaquist. "How did the kidnappers discover the tunnel system in the first place, if no one in your government knew of its existence?"

"Someone knew," Han Li responded. "In fact, the kidnappers knew not only about the tunnels, but also the room locations of their victims and the boundaries of the city's surveillance system. This kidnapping required an intense amount of planning based on classified information that should have been tightly controlled. Only someone at the upper levels of government would have that type of access."

"Then we have to assume that one or more senior Chinese

officials must be working with the Protectors. I'm going to tell Washington what you've uncovered. Then, after I get the disk, I'll look at the vans," Bonaquist said. As he stood to leave the restaurant, he handed Moretti and Han Li each a business card with his cell number. "I owe you both a huge favor for all you've done. If there's anything you need, you won't have to ask for it twice."

As he watched their waitress carrying a tray of food toward them, Moretti said, "I have a feeling that whoever's behind this will take exception to what we've discovered. They'll soon be issuing hunting licenses with our names on them."

"If they haven't done so already," added Han Li.

"There is that."

CHAPTER

7

Immediately after confirming that the president of the United States was missing, the Secret Service sent a small army of agents to supplement those already in place at the US Naval Observatory, the official residence of Vice President Charles Houck. An emergency meeting of the National Security Council was called, and at 1:00 a.m. the acting leader of the free world entered the White House Situation Room in the basement of the West Wing. Waiting for him was the president's national security adviser, select members of the president's Cabinet, the director of national intelligence, and the chairman of the Joint Chiefs of Staff.

Houck was six foot four, with closely cut salt-and-pepper hair and a lean physique from his days as quarterback of the Oklahoma Sooners national championship football team. He had become involved in politics after a final-game knee injury had ended his hopes for an NFL career. Two decades later he was governor of Oklahoma, followed by two terms in the US Senate before President Ballinger asked him to be his running mate. With Houck's reputation for being analytical and averse to making rash judgments, most people considered the sixty-three-year-old Midwesterner the next elected president of the United States.

When everyone was seated, Houck turned to Thomas Winegar and asked for his assessment of the abductions. In Washington, where "Go along to get along" was considered an everyday mantra, the director of national intelligence was a breath of fresh air for anyone who wanted politics removed from the advice they were being given. The Kansas City native, who spoke with a slight midwestern drawl, was looked upon as the Mark Twain of the National Security Council. It wasn't just his commonsense approach to complex issues and his good-natured humor, but also that his hair was completely white—though he was only in his fifties—with the slightly disheveled look of an Einstein or Twain. Winegar brought everyone up to date on what the intelligence community knew, ending with the fact that the Secret Service had found the president's watch and cell phone in his room. That meant, as Winegar explained, that Ballinger's subcutaneous location device was unable to effectively transmit his whereabouts.

"Do you believe the kidnappers knew about his implant?" Houck asked.

"I believe they assumed there was one," answered Winegar. "Subcutaneous location devices are common in world leaders, and a simple internet search will provide the basic details of how they operate. We presume that President Liu has a similar system, which was obviously neutralized by the kidnappers."

"To pull this off," Houck said, "the Protectors needed the assistance of at least one senior Chinese government official. Otherwise they couldn't have known the sleeping arrangements, positioning of security, and other particulars within and outside the Forbidden City."

"That's our assumption too," Winegar replied. "When planning the president's visit, the Secret Service was told by the Chinese Foreign Ministry that for security purposes and to prevent insider bickering, the top three officials in China's leadership hierarchy would determine who would spend the night within the Forbidden City and where they would be housed. They also indicated that they would release this information just three days before the gala."

"Since two of those three officials were kidnapped, that would seem to narrow our list of suspects to Second Vice Premier Ren Shi," said Jim Goodburn, the president's national security adviser. The Iowa native, who had been the Washington Redskins' punter when they won a Super Bowl, had later earned a doctorate in terrorism and cybersecurity from Georgetown. Then he served as a senior fellow at a Washington think tank for twenty-two years before President Ballinger asked him to join his administration. Goodburn was a straight shooter, definitely not prone to ambiguity when asked for his opinion.

"What you're saying is that this could have been a coup camouflaged to look like a kidnapping by the Protectors," said Robert Trowbridge. The six-foot-seven, square-jawed, silver-haired army general was chairman of the Joint Chiefs of Staff.

"If it was a coup, it couldn't have been carried out without assistance from the Chinese Communist Party," Goodburn replied. "No one is going to assume control in China without their buy-in. As the power behind the throne, they can effectively replace their country's president or any other government official at will, without the need for a coup. The world would be spoon-fed some fabricated story—perhaps that the current president is stepping down for health reasons."

Winegar said, "This is beginning to make sense. Not long ago, we learned that Ren Shi was going to retire and a new second vice premier was being named. We also have it on good authority that his retirement was not entirely voluntary."

"Which would mean," added Trowbridge, "that the kidnappers must kill President Liu, and by extension the rest of those abducted, in order to complete the transition of power."

"But why kidnap President Ballinger?" Houck asked.

Goodburn said, "I don't believe he was originally a target, because his invitation to the gala was extended only a few weeks ago. An operation of this magnitude would take substantially longer than that to plan. Whoever was behind this must have thought they had struck gold when it was announced that Ballinger was going. What better way to hide their real intent than to drag the United States into this?"

"Let's say, hypothetically speaking, that these assumptions are correct," Houck said. "We know how Ren Shi benefits, but what about the Protectors? Even if nothing happens to either president, they'll be hunted to the end of their days."

"I don't believe they benefit at all, sir," said Winegar. "And that's why I believe that the orange jumpsuits, the flag of the Protectors, and even the beheading was all just a front to point the finger at this terrorist group—which, in fact, has no connection to the kidnappings."

"So the Protectors are not part of this?" asked Houck.

"We have to consider that possibility," said Goodburn. "Afridi isn't stupid. He has to know that his group can't survive against two military giants such as the United States and China."

Houck saw that Secretary of Defense James Rosen, seated directly across from him, was squirming in his chair. Either he had to go to the bathroom or he had something he wanted to say. The vice president opted for the latter explanation and asked, "Do you have something to add, Jim?"

"I'm not buying any of this," the sixty-year-old former Marine Corps general said in his booming voice. "Neither Awalmir Afridi nor any of his lieutenants have denied the abductions, even though they've had ample time to do so. On the contrary, his followers are celebrating in the streets throughout the Middle East and Africa. That should tell us something. Afridi undoubtedly had a sect of the Protectors within China, of which we obviously weren't aware, who carried out his orders. He stands to gain big from this. If his demands are met, he'll control a large area of the Mideast and Africa."

"Then you don't believe there's been a coup?" Houck asked.

"I'm not saying that Ren Shi isn't involved," answered Rosen. "What I *am* saying is that Afridi is in this up to his neck. For crying out loud, his flag was hanging behind that poor bastard who was beheaded. How much more proof do we want? Do we need a signed affidavit?"

"Jim has a point," Houck said to Winegar, who was about to respond when Rosen's voice boomed out again.

"I have a question, sir. The kidnappers are asking for ransom. Will the United States break its long-standing rule of not negotiating with terrorists, even at the cost of the president's life?"

Houck leaned back in his chair, the stress evident upon his face, and looked around the conference table. No one spoke as they waited to hear his position and, by default, that of the US government. After an extended silence, he looked the secretary of defense directly in the eye and said, "The United States doesn't negotiate with terrorists. There will be no ransom. If we capitulate to these fanatics, it'll be open season on every American around the world."

"And if the unthinkable happens?" Rosen asked.

"If any harm comes to the president and we're able to identify those involved, then you have my permission to pursue them to the gates of hell and push them through." With that, Houck rose from the conference table and left the Situation Room.

Acting President Ren Shi had just finished addressing the nation on the abductions, concluding with a pronouncement, approved in advance by the Communist Party leadership, that the People's Republic of China did not negotiate with terrorists. Everything was going according to plan, with two exceptions—Moretti and Han Li. They had an uncanny ability to uncover what no one else could, threatening to upset a plan that had been in the making for more than a year.

Believing that they were exponentially more dangerous together than apart, Ren Shi decided that he needed to kill only one of them to stunt their effectiveness. Since Han Li was his country's premier assassin, he decided to eliminate Moretti. He picked up his office phone and told the person who answered that he wanted to see him and his partner immediately. Ren Shi felt a sense of calm as he set the handset back in its cradle. The men he had summoned had never failed to successfully complete any assignment they'd been given. If past performance was any indicator of the future, Moretti would be dead by morning.

The two heavily modified Sikorsky UH-60 Black Hawk helicopters were nearly inaudible as they skirted the treacherous mountains within the tribal area of North Waziristan. The radar-absorbent material that reshaped their surfaces, and lowered their radar signature to an almost undetectable level, allowed them to pass through Pakistani airspace undetected. When they arrived at their designated coordinates in the village of Razmak, they silently set down in pitch-black darkness not far from a modest brick dwelling.

As they exited the two aircraft, each of the twelve members of SEAL Team Six wore a black Crye Precision combat uniform, bulletproof vest, Salomon Quest combat boots, and four-tube night vision goggles. Strapped to each waist was a Sig Sauer P226 handgun, while in their hands each team member carried a suppressed, short-barrel HK MP7al submachine gun.

The brick residence they were approaching had no rear door, no gate, and no dogs or other animals that could alert anyone inside to their presence. The rules of engagement they'd been given indicated this mission would be weapons-free, meaning each team member had permission to fire on any target not recognized as friendly. Since they were Americans in the unfriendliest area for foreigners in Pakistan, this meant that they were pretty much cleared to fire on anyone they saw.

The first team member to reach the residence briefly studied the door and then affixed explosive breaching charges to the proper stress points. When the door was off its hinges, the team members would enter in predetermined order. The rear member carried a body bag in which the dwelling's primary occupant would be placed and taken to Bagram Airfield in Afghanistan for confirmation of his identity. From there it would be flown in a V-22 Osprey tiltrotor aircraft to an American carrier for burial at sea.

The team member who had placed the explosive charges turned his head away from the door, gave a warning through his helmet mic, and threw the detonation switch. An instant later the door blew off its hinges and eight men rushed inside. Two terrorists were sleeping on the floor when the explosion occurred, and both were cut down before they could comprehend what had happened. A shirtless man with a scruffy beard, who leaped from a side room with an AK-47 in his hands, came to a quick demise after being struck by a silent barrage of bullets. His body slammed against the wall behind him, leaving a wide red streak as he slid to the floor. Four team members stepped over him and rushed into the side room. A moment later there was a succession of two-round volleys, after which those four men left the side room to rejoin the rest of their team. Six suspected terrorists now lay dead, but not the one they'd been sent to kill. That meant that he was in the room to their left, the only room they hadn't entered.

Afridi had been awoken by the explosion of the breaching charges placed on the front door. He reached for the AK-47 that he kept beside him and checked to see that the safety was off, knowing that at any minute a Special Operations Team would enter his room. He flipped his bed on its side so that the double mattress would act as a bulletproof shield to absorb the high number of rounds that he expected to be directed at him. Sweat ran down his face, and his heart was beating so fast that he thought it would explode. Wondering how much longer it would be, he rested his weapon on the bed frame, pointing the barrel at the doorway so that he could drop anyone who entered.

A second later, the door blew off its hinges. Afridi went deaf from the explosive sound wave that slammed into his ears.

With his weapon on full auto, he pressed the trigger on the AK-47, expecting to kill anyone unlucky enough to be in front of him—but the gun didn't fire. He pressed the trigger again, with the same result. Afridi couldn't understand what was happening, but the only thing important now was survival. His bed was being peppered with bullets, which thankfully didn't penetrate the mattresses.

Reaching for his backup weapon on the floor beside his bed, Afridi saw one of the SEALs looking down at him. There was no emotion on the man's face as he brought his assault weapon to eye level and aimed it at Afridi's head. Afridi wanted to move, but he was frozen in place, as defenseless as a target on a practice range. As his eyes locked on the face of his executioner, time seemed to slow. He saw the SEAL squeeze the trigger and the muzzle flash as the projectile came at him and parted the center of his forehead.

Afridi woke up with a scream, and the men on guard outside his room scrambled through the door with their weapons drawn. He lay on his bed, breathing heavily and staring wild-eyed at the ceiling. Quickly composing himself, he sent his men away with a brusque command. But when they closed the door behind them, he dropped to his knees and prayed with all the religious fervor he could muster. Afridi couldn't help but wonder if Allah hadn't just sent him a glimpse of his future.

When they finished dinner, Han Li told Moretti that she'd come to his room in thirty minutes, after she'd had a chance to shower and change clothes. When she arrived, he could see that her face was drawn and her movements were slower than usual, mirroring the exhaustion that he too was experiencing.

He told her to take a seat on the edge of his bed, while he sat in a straight-back wooden desk chair a few feet away. "Any ideas?" he asked, conveying in those two words that he was at a dead end.

"Nothing of any consequence," said Han Li. "We could check for recent purchases of chloroform, but in a city the size of

Beijing, that would ultimately prove fruitless. Or we could have the government trace the license plates of all vehicles exiting either end of the mountain pass in the early-morning hours. The kidnappers have demonstrated that they're meticulous planners, so I suspect they used third-party vehicles just as they did with the vans, but it's worth a try."

As he sat in the stiff wooden chair, Moretti's back was beginning to spasm. He looked at the glass-faced minibar and an almost unquenchable desire to open one of the miniature Chivas Regals came over him. A month ago, he would have poured himself that drink. Since then, however, he'd worked hard to fight his alcoholic past and regain his self-respect, and he wasn't about to slip back into the abyss. Instead, he opened the fridge and grabbed two bottles of Evian, handing one to Han Li before uncapping his own.

"When I was on Air Force One," Moretti said, "the president briefed me on a Chinese defense manufacturer named Wang Lei. Are you familiar with him?"

"I know that he's the sole owner of Sovereign Industries, a private company that produces critical military hardware," said Han Li.

"Apparently one of our intelligence agencies has learned that Sovereign has produced an arsenal of cruise missiles that far exceeds what we consider to be the replenishment needs of your government. The United States believes that Wang Lei is stockpiling the missiles in anticipation of a major conflict. It wouldn't be a stretch to conclude that they would be used in a retaliatory strike following the deaths of the abductees."

"You're saying that every abductee will die?"

"That's a necessity," said Moretti. "If Wang Lei knew of the abductions ahead of time, he produced the missiles in anticipation of the conflict that he knew would ensue from these deaths."

"Sovereign Industries just completed the restoration of the

Forbidden City. It's possible that the tunnel system could have been discovered during the renovation," speculated Han Li.

"And Wang disclosed that information to the last man standing, the person who is now the most senior person in government," Moretti said.

"Ren Shi," Han Li replied softly, talking more to herself than to her partner. Then she continued, in a stronger voice, "They're childhood friends. It's rumored that Wang used his influence with senior Communist Party members, along with a great deal of money, to help Ren Shi ascend the ranks of government. Wang has never had a good relationship with President Liu. It's an open secret within the upper levels of government that he's been critical of Liu for not projecting China's military power abroad. Wang believes that by not doing so, our country is denied the respect and recognition it deserves."

"I don't know whether we're building a story to fit the situation," said Moretti, "or we've actually deduced who's behind this. I need to think this through. I'm going downstairs to get a cup of coffee. Care to join me?"

"No, I'm going to get some sleep. Let's meet here at six in the morning and go downstairs for breakfast," said Han Li.

After Han Li left, Moretti took the elevator to the lobby and got in line at Starbucks. It didn't seem to matter what time of day it was; the Chinese had a love affair with the Seattle-based company. It took ten minutes to work his way up to the barista and order a tall Pike Place Roast.

After getting his drink, Moretti saw two burly men, dressed in conservative business attire, get up from a brown leather couch in the lobby sitting area. Every other seat in the lobby was occupied, so he quickened his pace to get to the couch before anyone else noticed the vacant seats. The two burly men were carrying on a conversation with each other and apparently paying no attention to their surroundings. As they headed directly toward him, Moretti did his best—holding the piping hot coffee in his right hand—to avoid a collision, but one of the men clipped him. As Moretti juggled the coffee to keep it from flying out of his hand, he felt something scrape his neck. The man who had bumped into him stopped and profusely apologized in broken English, but Moretti told him to forget about it. Continuing to the couch, he took a seat and was immediately overcome by a wave of nausea. He set his cup of coffee on the floor, leaned back, closed his eyes, and hoped it would go away. But the nausea only got worse and was soon followed by a migraine headache.

Moretti knew that he needed to get up to his room and lie down. If he didn't feel better soon, he'd call for a doctor. As he slowly made his way to the elevator, his legs felt as if they were made of lead and he was having difficulty walking. He wondered if he should have stopped at the front desk and asked them to call a doctor. Now he wasn't sure he had enough strength to get there.

As he stepped inside the elevator, Moretti's legs felt like tree trunks and he was barely able to move. He pressed the second-floor button on the control panel and slumped back against the wooden paneling for support until the door reopened. It was fortunate that his room was not far away because he was starting to get sleepy. He had difficulty keeping his eyes open as he took baby steps down the hallway.

Then Moretti decided that he'd better go to Han Li's room for help. He used the wall for support to get to her door, but when he tried to knock, he lost all muscle control and his hands wouldn't move. A moment later he collapsed into the door, slid to the floor, and stopped breathing.

When Moretti looked up, the two fuzzy figures standing over him slowly came into focus and he recognized Han Li and Gao Hui.

"How are you feeling, Mr. Moretti?" Gao asked.

"Like I got run over by a train."

"That will pass as your blood chemistry returns to normal."

Standing behind Gao, Moretti could see a gray-haired man

with a stethoscope draped around his neck. "What happened to me?" he asked.

"Someone tried to poison you," Gao answered.

"I can't remember how I got here," said Moretti. "The last thing I recall was getting into the elevator in the lobby."

"You somehow made it to my room," Han Li told him. "I was getting ready to go to bed when I heard a noise outside my door. When I opened it, you were lying in the hall, unconscious and not breathing. As I was giving you CPR, I noticed a small florescent-purple cut on the side of your neck. That's when I knew you'd been poisoned because this toxin is administered by scratching the skin so that it penetrates the epidermis. The color goes away after the substance is fully absorbed into the body. Eventually the poison renders the victim semi-paralytic, taking away muscle functions such as breathing. It's impossible to detect the toxin in a postmortem toxicology screen because it decomposes into common body chemicals."

Moretti said, "You apparently know a lot about this poison."

Han Li didn't respond. So after a long pause, Moretti continued, "Since I'm alive, I take it there was an antidote."

"Yes," said Han Li. "I called Gao Hui, and he brought it."

"Why would someone want to kill me?" asked Moretti.

"They apparently fear that you have an uncanny ability to uncover what they hope to keep hidden for at least several more days," Gao said. "I believe they want to make sure that you aren't able to contribute anything further."

"Did you see who did this to you?" Han Li asked.

When he described the two burly men, Gao and Han Li looked at each other with a knowing glance.

Moretti said, "What?"

"We know the person they work for," Gao said. "In a way it explains a great deal. I'm going back to my office to find out who authorized the release of this poison, since that's above the authority of the two men whom you've just described."

"Be careful," Han Li cautioned. "If he knows you suspect him, he won't hesitate for a moment to have you killed."

Gao gave her a perfunctory nod, indicating that he understood.

When Gao and the doctor left, Moretti told Han Li that he needed to go back to his room. But as he started to get out of bed, she gently pushed him down and threw the covers back over him. "You're staying here tonight," she said. Her voice made it clear that the matter was settled. In short order, she took a pillow and blanket from the closet and placed them on the couch.

Just as Moretti was about to object, Han Li took off her robe, revealing black boy-short panties and a matching bra. The image of the scantily clad, five-foot-eleven, athletically built Han Li nearly took Moretti's breath away. He wondered how he could go through so many near-death experiences with her and still lack the courage to ask her on a real date. The only answer he could come up with … was that he was stupid. What he needed to do was walk to the couch, grab her hand, and lead her to bed. But in his present condition, he knew that wasn't going to work. Tonight, any romantic encounter would have to take place in his imagination.

CHAPTER

8

Moretti and Han Li were in the restaurant the following morning when Bonaquist arrived. One look at his haggard face and the deep circles under his eyes told them that he hadn't gotten any sleep. Something was wrong.

"They beheaded the minister of commerce," Bonaquist said, taking a chair at their table without waiting for an invitation. "The bastards put the video link on the internet. Then they released a statement that the minister was killed because the United States and China were moving too slowly on meeting their demands."

"I'd love to put a bullet between the eyes of the coward who beheaded him," Moretti said.

"You'd have to stand in line." Bonaquist was about to say something else, when one of his agents entered the restaurant and whispered something to him.

"Got to go. Acting President Houck wants an update," Bonaquist explained to Moretti and Han Li. "I'm sure there's nothing about the conversation that I'm going to enjoy, especially when I tell him that we've made zip progress since my last update." He got up from the table and left.

"This is starting to make sense," Moretti said as he cradled a cup of coffee in his hands. He still didn't feel a hundred percent, but he was rapidly gaining energy. The headache that had plagued him earlier that morning was almost gone.

"They're going to kill all the hostages," Han Li said, "just as you predicted."

"Yes, everyone needs to die. Otherwise their plan—for Ren Shi to become president and Wang Lei's business to expand as China becomes more militaristic—won't work."

Moretti waved to the waitress to refill his coffee cup. Then he took a sip of the steaming liquid and waited until she moved to another table before continuing. "I think it's time for us to take an offensive posture. No more playing defense. We take the fight to Ren Shi and Wang Lei."

"Since there's only the two of us, what do you propose?" asked Han Li.

"In the United States, we call it breaking and entering."

Ren Shi looked with scorn at the two burly men whose heads were bowed before him. If there was anyone else who could do the job and keep their mouth shut, he'd shoot both morons on the spot. But right then he had no alternative, so he needed to send them back to again try to kill Moretti.

Earlier that morning, one of Ren Shi's staff, who'd been assigned to keep an eye on Bonaquist, had reported that he'd seen the Secret Service agent in the hotel restaurant with Moretti and Han Li. That wasn't the call that Ren Shi had expected. Instead, he had wanted to hear that an American staying in the hotel had died after suffering a heart attack.

Ren Shi didn't understand how his two assassins had screwed up so badly. One of them said he'd scratched Moretti's neck with the razor-sharp edge of a special dispensing ring. Death should have been inevitable, since the only antidote was locked in a safe within the toxicology section of the Second Bureau. The only possible explanation was that the scratch hadn't penetrated the epidermis.

Taking a deep breath, Ren Shi tried to calm down. He was too close to success to be derailed by an interloper who shouldn't have been invited to the gala in the first place. This time the ground rules were going to change. He no longer cared whether Moretti's death was ruled to be from natural causes or a homicide. He'd send his assassins to try again. If Moretti wasn't dead by the end of the day, two members of his security team were going to have a fatal accident on the shooting range.

After his meeting with the National Security Council, Acting President Houck sat by himself in the Cabinet Room, still refusing to use the adjoining Oval Office out of respect for his friend. He considered the position that his secretary of defense had taken, which was directly opposite that of his national security adviser and the director of national intelligence. All three men had been persuasive in their arguments. Houck was leaning more toward siding with Rosen, given what he'd seen in the video and the fact that he believed the sadistic leader of this ruthless terrorist group was out to prove to the world that no one was safe from his reach.

There was a knock on the door of the Cabinet Room, and the Secret Service agent outside opened it to admit the chairman of the Joint Chiefs of Staff, whom Houck had summoned for a one-on-one meeting. He wanted there to be no misunderstanding about what would occur if there was confirmation that the president had been executed. Upon reflection, saying that he'd pursue whoever was responsible to the gates of hell wasn't specific enough.

If President Ballinger was killed, the United States needed to be prepared to take military action that would send a powerful message not only to those who carried out an attack, but also to any government that harbored them or provided them with support. The era of naive attempts of past administrations to understand and coddle terrorist groups who were no more than thugs and killers, under the guise of being politically correct, was over. From now on, the United States was a zero-tolerance nation that would respond to a terrorist attack at home or abroad with enough firepower to economically and militarily send those who carried out the attack, as well as their supporters, back to the Stone Age.

Wang Lei got out of the car and stretched. The drive from Beijing had taken nearly three hours, and his back was killing him. Kundek, who'd driven the entire way, seemed to be unaffected, although it was impossible to tell because of his usual emotionless expression. Under normal circumstances, Wang would have flown his company's helicopter, but using it when the military was frantically looking for the hostages would call undue attention to himself and invite too many questions.

He turned and looked at the broad expanse of dark green grass to his left, aware that below this bucolic landscape was a treacherous layer of rocks, boulders, ditches, holes, and a myriad of other natural hazards that made off-road travel extremely difficult. Wang had found this out the hard way, having broken an axle on his car when he had tried to take a short cut to the main road. The deceptive nature of this region extended also to its temperature, which could be Florida-pleasant during the day and Michigan-freezing at night. Only hard and disciplined people could survive here, which is why he'd always hired Mongolians from this area as his security guards.

Wang had first been attracted to this region, just over the Chinese border north of Beijing, because it was known to have vast deposits of coal, which he needed to fuel his manufacturing plants. After running the numbers, he had decided to buy his own mine and cut out the middleman. As it turned out, his company's energy costs dropped to a fraction of what they had been previously, but he also generated a great deal of money through the sale of coal to other companies.

His success at coal mining had led Wang to purchase a nearby mine that extracted copper, which was an important component of many of the electronic devices he manufactured. At first the mine's owner didn't want to sell; the price of copper was sky high, and he anticipated that it would stay that way for some time. However, after Kundek threw the owner down the mine shaft, Wang was able to persuade the man's heir to accept his offer. Wang bought the silver mine, his next purchase, solely as an investment. At that time, the market price of the precious metal had been so low that it was uneconomical to extract it from the earth. Owners of silver mines had been shuttering them, waiting to reopen their mines until the existing wholesale inventory was depleted and the price went back up. Those who were new to silver mining and leveraged their investment went out of business. Wang had taken advantage of one such person's inexperience and bought the dormant mine from the bank in a foreclosure sale.

Wang Lei closed the car door and followed Kundek away from the green pasture and toward the silver mine's two corrugated-steel buildings. They approached the building that was farthest from them where two men, each holding a Type 93 Chinese assault rifle, stood guard. One guard opened the door for Kundek while Wang waited outside.

The interior of the building was divided into two sections. On the left, consuming two-thirds of the space, was a large prison cell containing six metal cots. On each cot was a pillow and mattress that had probably been white at one time but were now charcoal in color. In the right-hand corner of the cell was a chemical toilet, whose stench permeated the interior of the building. Facing the cell from the outside was a gray metal desk with two matching chairs.

The hostages, lying on their beds, were dressed in orange jumpsuits. They no longer looked like the most powerful men in the world, but instead resembled a congregation of vagrants. Unshaven, their hair dirty and uncombed, they had the haggard look of men who knew that more bad things were going to happen to them.

They sat up when they saw the giant Mongolian enter the building, take a key from his pocket, and open the cell door.

Without saying a word, Kundek stepped between the cots of the senior vice premier and the minister of state security, grabbed each man by the arm, and led them out of the cell. No sooner had he relocked the cell and left the building, hostages in tow, then Wang entered.

"And how is everyone today?" asked the industrialist.

President Liu stared in disbelief as Wang walked to within three feet of the cell bars and smiled at him. "So you're the one behind this," he said, getting off his cot and approaching Wang. "How much were you paid to betray your country?"

"I admit that this was all my idea, but *paid*? *Betray*? You have it all wrong," argued Wang. "What I've done is change our country's future so that China will once again become a global leader."

"You'll have to explain how abducting two sitting presidents accomplishes that," President Liu said.

Rising from his cot and joining the Chinese president, President Ballinger added, "Whatever deal you or your intermediaries are trying to negotiate with the United States, it won't happen. We don't make deals with terrorists. And make no mistake about it—that's exactly what you and your accomplices are."

"You should also know that neither will our government negotiate, not even to save my life," President Liu said. "In the end you'll get nothing except the ire of two nations bent on killing you."

Wang replied, "Gentlemen, if you'll let me explain. For this endeavor to be successful, I'm counting on the unwillingness of the United States and China to negotiate. You're both going to die, but the ire of your two nations won't be directed at me. Blame will be directed toward the group I've so adeptly framed—the group that the world believes was responsible for the abductions."

Ballinger and Liu looked at each other with expressions of surprise.

"Neither of you actually understands what's going on or

the role you play," Wang said with an air of arrogance. "Let me explain what we've done."

"We?" Ballinger asked.

"As I said, the plan was mine," said Wang, "but I couldn't have succeeded without my partner."

"And who is that?" Liu demanded.

"I think I'll build the suspense for a while longer," Wang replied, clearly enjoying himself.

"What happened to the others who were in this cell?" asked Ballinger.

Wang replied bluntly, "They're dead."

"And Premier Chen and Minister Dai," Ballinger continued, "who were just taken?"

"Give them ten minutes," said Wang, "and they'll be beheaded just like the others."

"Beheaded?" Liu asked in disbelief.

"I apologize," said Wang. "I'm getting ahead of myself. Let me bring you up to date. After you were abducted and brought here, you were administered an opiate so that you would be conscious but not know or care what occurred around you. You were made to kneel beside a flag of the Protectors of Islam, and demands were made for your release. Therefore the world believes that it was this radical Islamic terrorist group who abducted you. And just to make it more convincing, your four roommates have been beheaded. I see the looks on your faces, but I assure you that I'm not a monster. I ordered that each of those men be given another dose of the opiate, so they wouldn't understand what was about to happen to them. It was the humane thing to do, after all. When all is said and done, it's the Protectors of Islam who will be hunted—not me."

"You're a psychopath and a murderer," Ballinger said.

"I'm not a psychopath, although I freely admit that I'm a murderer—but so are you. In fact, you're both mass murderers. Ordering drone strikes, sending troops into regions to kill people who don't agree with your views, choosing to sell weapons to anyone who will pay your price even if those weapons cause an untold number of deaths. I'd say we all paint with the same brush."

"You said our deaths would result in the reemergence of China as a global military power. How?" Liu asked.

"Think about what it is that limits our greatness. In the end, it comes down to two things: political will and money. Year after year you've limited the defense budget, giving our military only a third of the money they request," Wang said, looking at Liu. "This cripples China's ability to rival the military might and global reach of the United States. Because of decades of such thinking by inept leaders like you, no one fears us. Everyone knows that we have the political will to fight only on our own soil. Chinese citizens abroad can be killed, our embassies bombed, and our planes blown from the sky—and all we're likely to do is bring the matter before the United Nations. It's humiliating and unnecessary."

President Liu argued, "But our defense budget is a staggering $175 billion."

"While America's is more than $700 billion," replied Wang. "Centuries ago, when the United States was a country of Indians, we were the most formidable military power in the world. Our navy dominated the seas, and our army conquered whatever land we invaded. With the right leadership, we could return to those days of greatness. But we need a president with vision—and that's not you."

"Where do I fit in?" asked Ballinger, interrupting the tense exchange.

"You made it possible to significantly expand the geographic scope of our plan," Wang replied, his voice returning to a more conversational tone. "Before it was announced that you were attending the gala, our plan was to kidnap President Liu and several ministers, and then blame their abductions on the Philippine terrorist group Abu Sayyaf. They're notorious for their audacious kidnappings, ransom demands, and beheading their victims if their bounty isn't paid. As you know, there's currently a great deal of animosity between China and the Philippines over the ownership of various islands in the South China Sea."

Ballinger said, "So Abu Sayyaf would have been as easy to frame as the Protectors of Islam."

"Before your attendance was announced, we planned to use the tunnels to kidnap President Liu and other officials who have been adamant about not expanding our military budget," explained Wang. "We'd immediately behead one of the ministers to make our point. Then we would put out a statement in which Abu Sayyaf would claim responsibility and demand an exorbitant amount of ransom. All hostages would be killed, leaving President Liu for last. The Chinese people would demand immediate retribution, and we'd send our military to destroy Abu Sayyaf, irrespective of the denials that they'd most assuredly make. The Philippine government would respond, as any nation would, by telling us to leave their sovereign territory, threatening reprisals if we didn't. We'd ignore them, a war would ensue, and our military would seize control of that country. Part of the world would condemn us, and the rest would call it justifiable given that China was the aggrieved party."

"But those plans changed when you found out I was going to the gala," said Ballinger.

Wang explained, "I realized then that an opportunity had fallen into my lap. I could replace a regional conflict in the Philippines with an international conflict in the Middle East. Even better, instead of China conducting a military offensive by itself, it would partner with the United States. I couldn't pass up the opportunity. Think of the optics—China and the United States side by side, fighting the same group of terrorists. The world would come to respect China's military, and our government would quadruple the size of its budget to maintain a global military readiness."

ALAN REFKIN

"And you'll make a fortune from the sale of arms," added President Ballinger.

"I'm not in this for the money," insisted Wang. "I have more money than I can spend in two lifetimes. My goal is to transform my country into a global military superpower."

"You're a lunatic," Ballinger said. "You're willing to kill thousands of people just to restore the glory of the past."

"No, I'm a patriot. You may call me a lunatic, but what better way to protect a nation than to have a strong military that's able to fight our enemies before they get to our soil?" asked Wang.

President Liu asked, "Who within my government told you about the tunnels?"

"No one," Wang responded, turning his attention back to Liu. "They were discovered by accident. A little less than a year ago, as my company was renovating the Forbidden City, a backhoe driver was digging a three-foot-deep trench to bury a security camera cable. Everyone else had gone home for the day, but he needed to complete his work so that the electrical workers could install the camera the next morning. If he didn't finish, his pay would be docked. Somehow the driver's mind wandered and instead of digging to a depth of three feet, he excavated to a depth of almost seven, as he'd been told to do the previous day on a different job. At some point his bucket struck something solid. When he went to look, he saw that he'd broken through the ceiling of an old tunnel. He called his supervisor who, after inspection, phoned my assistant Kundek.

"When I arrived and saw what had been uncovered," continued Wang, "I sent the driver and his supervisor home with instructions not to tell anyone what they had seen. I then shut down all work within the Forbidden City for the next two days, so that I could take my time and inspect what had been unearthed. Kundek and I explored what we could of the tunnel system, going back for portable oxygen tanks when we found ourselves becoming asphyxiated. The seed of this plan came to me when we eventually discovered the secret entrances under the throne chairs and the tunnel exit. I had the driver and the supervisor killed to ensure that the tunnels remained a secret, and Kundek built a cover over the inadvertent breach and refilled the trench. While he was doing this, I mapped the tunnel network."

"You came up with the idea of a sleepover in the Forbidden City?" President Ballinger asked.

"It was a moment of inspiration," said Wang proudly. "I didn't present the idea to President Liu; someone else did that for me. But once the president endorsed the idea, my friend volunteered to take charge of assigning where everyone would stay. He made sure each person who was to be abducted slept in a throne room."

"Ren Shi is your accomplice?" Liu asked, as more a statement than a question.

"Who else could it have been? Since you were going to throw him out of office, getting his cooperation was easy. He and I have known each other since childhood, and I understand his thirst for power. I greased whatever palms were necessary to ensure Ren Shi's rise within the Party, knowing that one day my investment would be exponentially repaid. With the senior vice premier and you dead, he'll be the next president of China."

"Ren Shi is a traitor."

"That's true. Nevertheless, he will be the new leader of our country, remembered throughout history as the leader who vaulted us to greatness." Wang looked at his watch. "Now, if you gentlemen will excuse me, I'd like to observe these beheadings and make sure the camera angle is perfect." As he started to leave, he suddenly stopped and turned around. "Why don't I arrange for you both to see the video, so you'll know what to expect. After all, in two days you'll be the featured attraction for the largest internet audience in history."

CHAPTER

9

When they finished breakfast, Moretti and Han Li grabbed a Starbucks and sat at a small circular table at the edge of the lobby.

"You mentioned breaking and entering," Han Li said, looking around to make sure no one was within earshot.

"We need to break into Wang's Lei's office," said Moretti, "and see if we can find any evidence of his involvement in the abductions."

"Do you believe he'd be careless enough to keep that information lying around?"

"We won't know until we look. I'm hoping we'll get lucky and at least find a clue. We're sure as hell not going to uncover anything sitting here. How far away is his office?"

Han Li pointed at the large floor-to-ceiling windows to their left. "It's the large building in the distance."

Moretti could see the tall rectangular structure, faced with black reflective glass, that towered over the low-rise buildings surrounding it. "Since he's a defense contractor, security will probably be tight."

"That's a given," agreed Han Li.

"Let's agree that if we can't break into his office or don't find anything relating to the kidnapping once we're inside, plan B is to go to his house and interrogate him. When I introduce Wang

Lei to the joys of waterboarding, I guarantee that we'll find out everything he knows."

"If he knows anything."

"Yes, if he knows anything," Moretti reluctantly agreed, because at this point his involvement was pure speculation.

Han Li asked, "And the reason we don't go to his home and interrogate him now?"

"Because that's the last card we'd be able to play," explained Moretti. "It'll be messy, since we'll have to get past whatever electronic security he has in place and neutralize his bodyguards. And if it turns out, despite appearances, that he's not involved and we're captured or caught on a security camera, we're likely to spend the rest of our lives in a Chinese jail, assuming we live through the torture and attempts to kill us in prison." Changing the subject, he asked, "What do we know about the interior of the headquarters building?"

Han Li accessed the internet browser on her cell phone, found Sovereign Industries, and looked through the corporate website. There she found an informational drawing showing the physical locations of numerous departments and senior management within the high-rise. She showed this to Moretti.

"I believe I know how we can get in," Moretti said, with a grin on his face. "I think it's time that you get a job."

From a distance, the two burly men watched Moretti and Han Li get into a taxi and leave the hotel. They took the next cab in line, following their targets to Wangfujing Street, the spine of the busiest commercial shopping area in Beijing.

Over the next half hour Moretti and Han Li went in and out of several stores, making purchases in three of them. After they'd left the last store, they walked down a small side street that ran perpendicular to the busy thoroughfare. The burly men followed, but kept their distance. The narrow street was cordoned off with older apartment buildings of weathered red brick and air-conditioning units that filled window openings. Since nearly everyone was at work, the residential area was devoid of people and vehicle traffic. Moretti and Han Li continued at a leisurely pace, strolling deeper into the working-class neighborhood.

"I must be at the top of Ren Shi's shit list for him to send those two goons back for another try," Moretti said. "It's a good thing you noticed them at the hotel."

"It's hard for men that size to blend in," said Han Li. As they turned a corner, she caught a glimpse of them in her peripheral vision. "They've picked up their pace, so it won't be long."

"What do you want to do?" asked Moretti.

Han Li said, "I'll cut down this side street and come around behind them. If they attack before I return, hold them off." She handed him her plastic bag, crossed the street, and disappeared.

Moretti didn't know how he was going to fend off two assassins, especially since he had no weapon. With Han Li gone, he had little choice but to continue walking and hope she'd arrive in time. But that hope quickly faded when he heard rapidly approaching footsteps behind him. He was in a quandary about whether he should turn and face the two men or increase his pace to give Han Li additional time. Having seen her martial arts skills, he elected the latter.

Moretti quickened and extended his stride, but the burly men did the same. Soon he could hear their footsteps only a few yards behind him. Where was Han Li? He thought about running, but his back had tightened so much that he could barely maintain his current pace. Seeing no alternative, he dropped the plastic bags and turned to face his pursuers.

The two men drew five-inch knives from under their sleeves and slowly inched Moretti backward until he was against a ten-foot-high redbrick wall. At that point one of the burly men lunged forward. As a former Army Ranger, Moretti had received extensive training in hand-to-hand combat and was involved in more than his share of knife fights while deployed in the Middle East. He quickly moved aside, as the blade passed just in front of his face, and then grabbed the man's hand in a viselike grip. At the same time, he brought his knee up as hard as he could into his assailant's groin, ending the altercation with a roundhouse to the jaw. The burly man, who weighed more than 250 pounds, crumpled to the sidewalk. His partner then backed away, apparently realizing that this adversary was more formidable than expected.

Moretti didn't get a sense of relief from what he'd just done because, directly in front of him, the other burly man was bending his wrist back in preparation for throwing his knife. Moretti knew there was no possibility he'd be able to reach the person before he released the blade and that the knife would cover the distance between them in the blink of an eye. Making a split-second decision, he decided to leap to the side. If his timing was correct, the blade would impact the wall behind him, and if not, he'd be dead. Unfortunately, just as he transferred weight to his right leg, his lower back, which had become increasingly tense all day, picked that moment to spasm and he collapsed onto the ground. Unable to get up he expected to feel, at any moment, the blade burying itself within him. Instead, he heard a loud crack followed by the sound of a body hitting the ground. Looking in front of him he saw Han Li standing over the burly man, who had the right side of his skull caved in.

Moretti extended his arm so that Han Li could help him stand. Instead, she raced past it. As he turned to see where she was going, he saw that the other burly man held a knife inches from him. With no time to react he watched as Han Li thrust the palm of her hand into the man's throat with enough force to instantly crush his larynx and deny his body life-sustaining air.

Han Li helped Moretti to his feet and then searched both men. The only items they carried were wallets, which she placed in her jacket pocket before retrieving the plastic shopping bags. Then she and Moretti made their way back to Wangfujing Street, hailed a taxi to their hotel, and went directly upstairs to Moretti's room.

"Let's see what we have," Han Li said, taking a seat on the edge of the bed and removing the brown leather wallets from her pocket. Inside the first was a small amount of cash, a credit card, national and government IDs, and a folded piece of paper.

"What does it say?" Moretti asked, taking a seat beside her and watching her unfold the paper.

"It's an authorization from Ren Shi, ordering the full cooperation of whoever is presented with this letter."

Moretti asked, "Is that common?"

"Not in my experience." Han Li opened the second wallet, finding similar contents and the same authorization letter.

"It would seem," said Moretti, "that Ren Shi wants us dead. If that's the case, he'll continue to throw assassins at us until he achieves that end."

"Does that mean it's time for breaking and entering?"

"Oh yeah."

At 4:45 that afternoon, Han Li entered the lobby of the Sovereign Industries building. Looking through a digital directory, she confirmed that the offices of both the human resources director and Wang Lei were at the top of the building on the fiftieth floor. Taking the elevator, she went through a set of glass doors and asked the receptionist for an employment application. The receptionist told her that only the executive offices were on this floor and that the office that handled new hires, which would close in just forty minutes, was five floors below, and she gave Han Li the name of the person to contact. Han Li started to return to the elevator, but then she turned back and asked the receptionist where she could find a restroom. She was directed to go past the elevator and about three-quarters of the way down the hallway to her right.

When she entered the ladies' room, Han Li phoned Moretti. Five minutes later, he got off the elevator and went into the adjoining men's restroom. Han Li had earlier told him that

Chinese businesses almost always placed their bathrooms away from the employees' working area and that she was relatively certain that Sovereign would follow that same practice. If not, they were back to plan B—kidnapping Wang Lei—because plan A required unobstructed access to a room that would not have an alarm in it.

Moretti was wearing a backpack containing the items they'd purchased earlier that day. No one else was in the men's room, a fact that he confirmed by inspecting the individual stalls. He looked at the drop ceiling, thankful that it was suspended rather than drywall. Otherwise he'd have needed to use his newly purchased saw to cut a hole. He pushed a nearby trash receptacle up to the sink, climbed up, and pushed back one of the white acoustical ceiling tiles. Then he poked his head into the opening, turned on his flashlight, and looked around.

The aluminum framework supporting the ceiling tiles, intermingled between a grid of wide structural girders and H-beams, extended as far as Moretti could see. Han Li was standing on the steel support immediately to his right, extending her hand to help him through the opening. Before the most recent encounter with the two burly men, he would have ignored her offer of assistance. But now, with his back muscles still tight and painful, he reached up and grabbed hold of the girder with his left hand and Han Li's arm with his right, pulling himself up and onto the beam. Once he was on solid footing, Han Li replaced the ceiling tile.

"Thanks," Moretti said, clearly embarrassed that he had needed help.

They sat down on opposite sides of an H-beam, using their backpacks as cushions against the hard steel. They knew they were in for a long wait, since they couldn't enter the executive offices until the last employee left. Given that Chinese workers were notorious for working late to impress upon their employers their loyalty and commitment to their jobs, Moretti and Han Li could be waiting for several hours.

Earlier that afternoon, they'd discussed the option of entering the building later, but there were too many variables, including the risk of arriving after the office was closed for business. They assumed that they would have then needed an employee ID and possibly a key to get past lobby security and use the elevator or stairs. Moretti had seen a key receptacle when he pushed the button for the fiftieth floor.

The hours slowly rolled by, but finally it was time. At ten o'clock that evening, it had been forty-five minutes since they'd last heard the elevator doors chime open.

One of the unknowns was whether there were motion or heat sensors. Han Li hadn't see any when she was at the reception desk, but that didn't mean they didn't exist. Moretti and Han Li had agreed that if sensors were present and operational, they were wasting their time, so the first thing they needed to do was test for them. If they set off one or more sensors, they might have a slim chance of escaping detection by hiding in the ceiling till morning.

Moretti used his flashlight to light the beam they were on, and they walked along it until they were sure they were over the executive office space. Han Li knelt and removed one of the ceiling tiles, then lowered her head into the office space. She could see the red glow of the alarm panel behind a plant in the far corner, just to the right as one entered the office. She waved one arm while holding on to Moretti's hand with the other, and thirty seconds later raised her body back into the ceiling space.

"We'll know soon enough," Moretti said, as they waited to see if a silent alarm had been triggered. Twenty minutes later, nothing had happened, so they concluded that there were no internal sensors.

While Han Li held the flashlight, Moretti took a length of nylon rope from his backpack, tied it to the beam, and lowered himself ten feet to the floor. Han Li then untied the knot and let the rope fall to him, and he stuffed it into his backpack. Making sure the ceiling square was nearly in place, Han Li dropped to the floor, and as she did so, the tile settled neatly back into position.

They were adjacent to the reception desk, behind which was a large glass-enclosed conference room. Lining the two exterior walls were rows of private offices. All were the same size except for the one in the corner, which had a double-door entry. Moretti and Han Li decided to start there.

They didn't expect to find the corner office unlocked. The good news was that the dead bolt was cheap, and Han Li used her picks to defeat it in less than a minute. The space they entered was rectangular, measuring fifteen by forty feet. To the far left was a round teak conference table with four high-back black leather chairs evenly spaced around it. Affixed to the wall behind the table was a large unframed map of China and Inner Mongolia. Thirty blue pins were stuck into black dots designating Chinese cities, and three red pins were clustered together in the southernmost part of Inner Mongolia—apparently in the middle of nowhere. To the right of the table was another door, which led to a small kitchen. Moretti inspected the kitchen and then returned to the office. The center of attention on the other side of the room was a black lacquer desk with a deeply padded black leather chair.

"Why don't you go through his desk while I take a look around," Moretti suggested.

Han Li agreed, since he didn't read Chinese and wouldn't know which papers were important.

Moretti went to the other end of the office and inspected the map, trying to determine what the pins represented. Drawing a blank, he snapped several pictures of it with his cell phone before rejoining Han Li.

"There's nothing in this desk that's going to help us," she said, the disappointment apparent in her voice.

"I'm not surprised," said Moretti. "This building doesn't have the security you'd associate with a defense contractor. My guess is that what's here is strictly administrative, and the sensitive information on weapons systems, shipments, and customers is at the manufacturing sites, where they're bound to have more stringent access and monitoring procedures."

"Then we're wasting our time. Let's leave before anyone sees us."

As if on cue, they heard the familiar chirp of the security system being disarmed. Moretti quickly shut off the lights and relocked the office door. Using his flashlight, he led Han Li into the small kitchen, closing the door behind them just as they heard the office door open.

When Kundek and Wang walked into the office, the Mongolian broke left and took a seat at the teak table, while Wang went to his desk and placed the computer he removed from his briefcase on its glassy black surface. Using a simple mail transfer protocol (SMTP) service that a member of his IT department had set up, he anonymized his outgoing email, scrubbing it of any identifying information that could lead someone to him. It would have been quicker to use the wireless internet connection at his mine, but that connection had proven to be spotty and unreliable—a common problem in that region of Inner Mongolia.

When he finished posting the video of the beheadings, along with a printed message, Wang turned off his computer and returned it to his briefcase. He was tired from stress and a lack of sleep. He'd given up smoking a dozen times, but he couldn't seem to permanently kick the habit he'd picked up as a teenager. Whenever he was tense and needed to relax, he'd light up his special blend of rich tobaccos and inhale the smoke deep into his lungs. Whether it was psychological or physical, smoking always seemed to calm him down.

When Wang opened the top drawer of his desk to retrieve his cigarettes and lighter, he noticed that his papers, which he routinely kept in a neat stack, were slightly askew. Documents in the other drawers were also in slight disarray. Obsessive-compulsive about keeping his paperwork in perfect alignment, he suspected that someone had searched his office. Then he and Kundek both heard a faint noise come from the kitchen. Kundek drew his gun from the small of his back, threw open the kitchen door, and turned on the interior light. Seeing no one, and knowing the space had no rear exit, he began searching the cabinets and storage closet. When he finished, he shook his head to Wang, who was standing in the doorway.

The industrialist turned and went back to his desk. As Kundek was about to follow, he noticed several white particles scattered at his feet. If the carpet hadn't been dark brown, they would have gone unnoticed. He bent down and picked up one of the white specks, then looked up at the ceiling and saw that the corner of the tile above him was chipped. Retrieving a ladder from the back of the kitchen, Kundek pushed aside the damaged tile and poked his head into the open space. Using the Mag Light app on his phone, he looked around—not that he expected to see anyone. He already knew who'd been there.

Han Li followed Moretti into the ladies' room, dropping below the ceiling and replacing the tile a heartbeat before Kundek turned the Mag Light in their direction. Moving quickly, they ran into the hall. Taking the elevator was out because they were fairly certain that the guard had a screen that showed the movement of elevators within the building. Without employee IDs, they'd be questioned about what they were doing in the building at such a late hour. So they decided to take the staircase. Twenty minutes later and dripping with sweat, they entered the parking garage and found a side exit that led to the street.

When they stopped running, Moretti's back muscles tightened and made it difficult for him to walk, so it took longer than anticipated to return to the hotel. As he and Han Li finally entered the lobby, they decided to go to his room to regroup, since they were once again at a familiar place—square one. Walking into his room, Han Li went to the refreshment counter to get a bottle of water, while Moretti dropped his backpack on the floor and bent over, trying to loosen his muscles by attempting to touch his toes.

Neither of them saw Kundek come out of the walk-in closet behind them. The Mongolian struck Moretti on the side of the head with his gun. When Han Li turned at the sound of her partner's body hitting the floor, she saw Kundek's gun pointed at her. As he kept his weapon centered on her chest, he removed four flex ties from his left jacket pocket and tossed them at her feet.

"Tighten one pair around his wrists and one around his ankles. Then do the same to yourself," Kundek said in a monotone. After she'd finished, he further tightened them to the point of almost cutting off the circulation in their hands and feet. He then slapped Moretti on the side of his face, bringing him back to consciousness. "I'm glad you're awake," Kundek said. "I wouldn't want you to miss your death."

Moretti blinked several times, trying to figure out if he was dreaming. When he was awake enough to determine that he wasn't, mainly because his arms and legs were bound, he sat up against the side of the bed and faced Kundek. "Why kill us?" he asked, as he watched the Mongolian remove a suppressor from his jacket pocket and screw it onto the end of his gun. "We don't know anything."

"You know a great deal, but fortunately you haven't been able to piece it together," Kundek said, as he racked the slide on his Glock 38. "I'm here to ensure that you never get that opportunity." Extending his arm, the Kundek looked Moretti in the eye and aimed the gun at the center of his forehead. Watching his killer's finger gradually tighten on the trigger, Moretti braced for the bullet's impact.

"Moretti, it's Bonaquist. Open up," the agent said, pounding on his hotel room door. "I need to talk to you now. There's another video on the internet, and I need to pick your brain again before I speak to Washington."

Instinctively turning toward the sound of the pounding, Kundek fired four rounds through the door. Then he quickly threw it open, wanting to make sure that the Secret Service agent, whom he knew by name, was dead. Instead, he saw his intended victim several yards to his left with his back flat against the wall. Even worse, Bonaquist had his gun pointed directly at him.

Kundek dove to the floor as two rounds went by his head close enough for him to feel their passage. The next two rounds slammed into the wall beside the Mongolian as he ran across the hall and opened the stairwell door. Scrambling down one flight of stairs to the outside exit just off the lobby, he ran through the rear parking lot with every bit of speed his huge frame could muster. Safely reaching the thick stand of trees at the perimeter of the property, he then cautiously worked his way back to the Sovereign Industries building.

"Did he get away?" Moretti asked Bonaquist.

"You think it'd be impossible to miss someone that big," Bonaquist said, chastising himself for not being able to put a bullet into such a large target. "I need to get my eyes checked. Do you know who that was?" the agent asked as he took a knife from his pocket and cut the flex ties binding Moretti and Han Li.

"I don't know his name," answered Moretti, "but I'm fairly sure he works for Wang Lei."

"The military industrialist?" asked Bonaquist.

Moretti motioned Bonaquist to the desk chair. "Take a seat. I think you'll find that what I'm about to tell you is possibly relevant to what's happened here tonight. On our flight from the States to Beijing, President Ballinger gave me a briefing on Wang Lei, which I was subsequently ordered to keep to myself. However, considering what's happened, I believe that admonition no longer applies."

Moretti then went on to recount what the president of the United States had told him and why he believed Wang Lei and Ren Shi were working in concert. He told Bonaquist how he had been poisoned and later attacked by the two burly men, and that he and Han Li had broken into Sovereign Industries to try to find out where the cruise missiles were shipped. He finished by explaining that their break-in at Sovereign had undoubtedly prompted the subsequent attack in his hotel room.

"You said that the person who tried to kill you a few minutes ago worked for Wang Lei?" asked Bonaquist.

"I have to assume so," said Moretti, "since he tried to kill us shortly after we broke into Wang's office. I also suspect he's one of the kidnappers. If you look at the video, you'll see a person matching his body profile leaving the tunnel."

"Come to think of it, he's also the same build as the executioner in the videos," Bonaquist added.

"He's not much of a talker, but just as he was about to kill me, I asked him why he wanted me dead since I really don't know anything. His answer was that I know a great deal but haven't been able to piece everything together. That came as a surprise because I didn't think that Han Li and I had uncovered anything that would lead us to the whereabouts of the presidents."

Bonaquist said, "Maybe he's assuming that you know more than you actually do."

"Maybe," agreed Moretti.

"Why didn't you tell me at breakfast that you'd been poisoned?" asked Bonaquist.

"Sorry, but you were called away before I had a chance," Moretti replied. "And I didn't want to tell you about the second attempt on my life, because we were getting ready to bust into Wang Lei's office at Sovereign Industries. I was afraid that you might put me under protective surveillance if you found out."

"You got that right. You and Han Li are walking targets. If you weren't the source of all my leads, I'd say leave Beijing. But since you are, I'm grateful that you're staying." Bonaquist turned to leave, but then suddenly snapped his fingers and did an about-face. "Oh, I almost forgot why I came to your room in the first place." His demeanor turned grim in anticipation of what he was about to say. "They beheaded the minister of commerce and the senior vice premier. A message appeared in the video, over their decapitated bodies, indicating that this execution was intended to demonstrate how serious they are about their deadline."

"It's not about the deadline," Han Li said. "Ren Shi wants the presidency and Wang Lei is going to make sure he gets it, which means that both presidents must be killed."

"If that happens, Americans will demand that the Protectors of Islam be erased from the planet," said Moretti.

"And the Chinese people will want their revenge also," Han Li added. "This is probably the reason Wang escalated his production of cruise missiles, anticipating the military retaliation that would ensue in response to the death of President Liu."

If Bonaquist seemed surprised at what they'd said, he didn't show it. "I'll update Washington and give them your take on Ren Shi and Wang Lei," said Bonaquist as he rose from his chair. "You're lightning rods for attracting trouble. Call me at any time if you need the cavalry."

After he left, Moretti pulled the cell phone from his pocket and sat on the edge of the bed. "Look at this," he said, bringing up the image he'd taken of the map in Wang Lei's office. He enlarged it as Han Li sat beside him. "This is the map next to the table in Wang's office. I'm guessing that the pins represent the various locations of Sovereign Industry offices or facilities. The blue ones are stuck in major cities throughout the country, such as Beijing. But what interests me are the red pins because they're in the middle of nothing on the map. Any idea of what's there?"

"Inner Mongolia," answered Han Li. "I've never been there, but from what I've heard, the area is mostly mining, wind turbines, and livestock."

"If someone wanted to hide six abductees from prying eyes, that just might be the perfect place. How far is it from here?"

"The border is less than a two-hour drive. But saying the

presidents are there is a stretch, given that all you're going on is three pins in map."

"Consider this. Hiding the presidents in Beijing would be very risky, with everyone on the lookout for anything the least bit suspicious. On the other hand, Inner Mongolia is not only a short drive from here, but it's probably also the last place anyone would think of looking."

"You might be right," conceded Han Li. "Did you get a good look at the person who tried to kill us?"

"Which one are you referring to? There have been three so far."

"The huge man who was waiting for us in this hotel room. To an American, all Asians look the same. But to an Asian, the distinctions are obvious. His facial features were undeniably Mongolian."

"Maybe the pieces of this puzzle are starting to come together. If you think about it, Inner Mongolia would be the perfect place to hide two world leaders. Who would think to look there?"

"The downside for us," cautioned Han Li, "is that if we're wrong, we'll have no time to get back here and evaluate other alternatives."

"As it happens, that really doesn't matter," Moretti said.

"Why not?"

"Because we haven't any alternatives."

CHAPTER

10

A cting President Charles Houck slowly put the phone back in its cradle, ending his call with Acting President Ren Shi. They'd agreed on the execution time, or e-hour, for an all-out assault on the Protectors of Islam. If Ballinger and Liu were killed, the Pentagon would launch 250 cruise missiles against the radical Islamic group's locations in six Middle Eastern countries at 6:30 p.m. Beijing time. The Chinese leader confirmed that he'd set the same e-hour for their military to commence their missile assault against the group's strongholds in Africa.

Houck had earlier questioned General Trowbridge about the need for such a large number of missiles, and the general had explained that the mountainous terrain and geographical distribution of the group across the Middle East necessitated such a quantity. Houck understood that despite the pinpoint accuracy of the weapons, tens of thousands would die—and a significant percentage would be innocent civilians whose only crime was being in the wrong place at the wrong time. The thought of their deaths made him want to throw up, but there was no other way to successfully strike a mortal blow at this group.

Afridi had the cowardly practice of locating most of his bases of operation and much of his stockpile of weapons within civilian areas. He believed the United States and other Western countries would never attack his installations or followers when there was

ALAN REFKIN

a chance of noncombatant casualties. Charles Houck, however, was changing the rules of engagement.

The only potential problem Hauck foresaw was that, according to Trowbridge, no one knew exactly where Awalmir Afridi was hiding. The general believed the terrorist leader was in North Waziristan taking refuge among the tribal leaders, who traditionally protected him from outsiders, but there was absolutely no guarantee of that. Trowbridge told Houck that Afridi's body, or what remained of it, might never be found, but Houck didn't care. In the end, Afridi would be dead and a message would have been delivered to every terrorist on the planet: if you fuck with the United States, start writing your obituary.

After watching the video of the latest beheadings, Afridi slammed the cover of his computer down so hard that he cracked the screen. More than anything he had ever wished for in his entire life, he wanted to wrap his hands around the neck of whoever was responsible for these abductions and squeeze the last breath of life from him. Not only had this idiot usurped his leadership authority, but these actions would cause the Saudis, Kuwaitis, Iranians, and others to unify and turn against him if the Americans attacked his followers in their countries.

These countries rewarded him handsomely for keeping his terrorist activities outside their borders and leaving their governments alone. The hundreds of millions they paid into his coffers had enabled him to buy arms and equipment, bribe officials, pay his soldiers, and expand his empire. And as long as he hadn't attacked America or its foreign interests, the United States had been consistent in limiting its actions to saber-rattling rhetoric and intermittent drone strikes. But the abduction of the American president had destroyed this fragile equilibrium.

In twelve hours, if this unnamed and faceless moron carried out his threat, which he fully believed would happen, the United States would come after him with every bit of conventional firepower they possessed. He'd heard from his friends in Pakistan and Saudi Arabia that the United States had already amassed a great many ships in the Gulf, as well as submarines capable of launching cruise missiles. In the past, this would have been viewed as a show of force meant to intimidate, rather than a realistic threat of attack—but not this time. When the American president was beheaded, Afridi knew that the most lethal superpower on the face of the planet would be coming after him.

His friends also told him that the Chinese were planning to send aircraft with cruise missiles to Africa to attack his strongholds on the continent, but Afridi didn't care about that. His presence in Africa was mainly for show. Many African leaders were so corrupt that they gladly paid to be left alone, so that they could continue their financial pillage of their own countries.

Afridi had directed some of his most trusted followers to begin taking arms and supplies, including clothing, to the cave that had been his family's secret hiding place for generations. Well hidden behind large outcroppings of rock, the cave's numerous entrances were almost impossible to spot from either the ground or the air. Afridi had first visited the cave as a child, and its vast internal labyrinth had been filled with illegal arms that were being sold to anyone who could afford them. His father had been a businessman, not an idealist.

Now Afridi was about to use his hiding place for a very different reason—to survive an attack by a superpower bent on revenge. In the aftermath of the beheading of the two presidents, he wouldn't be able to stay in one location long or he'd be discovered and killed, just like Osama bin Laden had been. Thankfully, Afridi had more than $1 billion deposited in various banks around the world and an escape plan to leave the country when the time came.

Afridi looked at his home one last time, and then walked to the waiting SUV. Two hours later, they'd gone less than fifteen miles. The vehicle stopped at the end of a long and narrow dirt path. He stepped out and stretched, looking at the rugged mountains and boulder-strewn valleys he'd known since childhood. Meanwhile the driver took the car into a nearby ravine and cut the adjoining brush to cover it.

The path to the cave was not obvious, so Afridi took the lead in guiding those with him over the rocky terrain and up steep paths to the main entrance. Turning around, he looked at North Waziristan in the distance and wondered if he'd live to visit it again. Then, suddenly realizing that everyone had stopped and was looking at him, he pushed those thoughts aside. Entering the cave, he grabbed one of the electric lanterns off the dirt floor, turned it on, and began inspecting the interior to ensure that the arms and supplies he'd sent ahead were there.

Bonaquist phoned Moretti in his room and asked that he and Han Li meet him in a recessed alcove just down from the Starbucks counter. When they arrived, a venti Pike Place Roast and a similar-sized green tea were on the table where the Secret Service agent was sitting.

"Thanks, I needed this," Moretti said. He grabbed the coffee and took a seat, while Han Li slid her tea in front of the chair next to him.

Bonaquist took a couple of sips from his venti caramel macchiato before placing the cup back on the table. Forgoing small talk, he started right in. "I just received a call from the director of the Secret Service. It seems that Ren Shi has informed the State Department that my agents and I are to stay away from Wang Lei and his company. He also asked that if any of us sees you, we're to detain you until someone from the People's Liberation Army arrives—and the director has ordered me to do that."

"What about Han Li?" asked Moretti.

"I was told that the Chinese government would deal with her separately," explained Bonaquist. "I got the feeling that they were going straight to your hotel rooms, which is why we're sitting here and having this discussion."

Moretti said, "Sounds like they want to throw us in jail so that we can't interfere. What do you think?"

"I think it's all bullshit," said Bonaquist. "After what you told me last night, I have little doubt that Wang Lei and Ren Shi are conspiring together and that they're afraid that you and Han Li will expose their involvement."

"I have no intention of letting them arrest me," said Moretti.

"Neither do I," Han Li added.

"I didn't expect either of you to roll over. Speaking frankly, I believe that you're our only chance of finding the presidents. I'm not going to detain you, but you both have a significant problem," Bonaquist said, looking over Moretti's head.

"Which is?" asked Moretti.

"Him." Bonaquist pointed to Yan He, who had just arrived with four of his men.

"Mr. Moretti," the lieutenant colonel said as his soldiers surrounded the table. "I've been ordered to arrest you and Han Li for breaking into the offices of Sovereign Industries. Please come with me." Although his words were polite enough, his authoritarian voice indicated that he would not tolerate any delay or discussion.

"Colonel," objected Bonaquist, "this man is a United States citizen."

"Yes, a US citizen who has broken Chinese law." With a head gesture, Yan He signaled his men to take Moretti and Han Li into custody.

In the blink of an eye Han Li hit the guard to her right with a sideswipe to the jaw, causing him to black out. The guard to her left fared no better; she struck his jaw with an uppercut, rendering him unconscious before he collapsed to the floor. Neither as creative nor as skilled in the martial arts as Han Li, Moretti was all about brute force. When he saw her go on the attack, he grabbed the necks of the soldiers on either side of him and smashed their heads together, causing them to collapse to the floor. Yan He was drawing his gun when Han Li's foot crashed into his stomach and doubled him over. When she followed with a temple punch between the colonel's hairline and eyebrow, he immediately blacked out as his brain slammed against his skull lining.

"You two better get out of here," said Bonaquist as he looked at the five bodies. "I'll see if I can buy you some time. We've got a little less than eight hours before both presidents are scheduled to be executed. Make sure that doesn't happen."

Moretti wanted to say something heroic or patriotic, but he couldn't think of anything. Instead, he nodded and followed Han Li out of the hotel.

Bonaquist used his cell phone to call one of his agents, who arrived less than a minute later.

"What the hell happened here?" the agent said, looking at the five soldiers Bonaquist had dragged into the back of the alcove.

"Never mind that. Go to my room and bring me the large emergency medical kit," Bonaquist said, handing his keycard to the agent. "Get back here as quickly as you can."

It was still early, and the morning hotel crowd at Starbucks had yet to arrive. Thankfully the alcove was not readily visible, except from the side door through which Yan He and his men had come. But it was only a matter of time until someone came along.

The agent returned with the ten-pound box of medical supplies and placed it next to the unconscious soldiers, whereupon Bonaquist removed two large vials and five syringes. After siphoning fluid from the glass bottles, he injected each of the soldiers.

"What did you give them?" asked the agent.

"A sedative that will knock them out for seven or eight hours. Get some help down here before someone sees us. We'll take Lieutenant Colonel He to my room and the other soldiers to yours. Put the Do Not Disturb sign on the door, and make sure you're inside the room with them at all times. I'll take full responsibility for what's happened. You're just following orders."

"Why are you risking your career and probably jail time by doing this?"

"Because if I didn't," said Bonaquist, "there'd be no chance of saving the president of the United States."

Ren Shi looked at his watch. It wouldn't be long before the presidents were beheaded, and then he was all but certain to be named president. Now that he had ordered that Moretti and Han Li be arrested, he felt a sense of serenity. Their investigative instincts and ability to piece together loosely related facts were uncanny. When Wang had phoned and told him about the break-in, Ren Shi had panicked. He wasn't sure how much those two troublemakers knew about his partner's involvement or his own complicity. He was afraid that if he didn't take them out of the equation and silence them, everything would fall apart.

Ren Shi had phoned the US ambassador to China and requested his assistance. On reflection, he'd probably been too impulsive in making that call. He should have just arrested Han Li and Moretti before the Americans knew what was happening, but it was too late for that now.

Even though the Americans now knew that Moretti was going to be arrested, they didn't know that he'd be taken to the Black Prison. Beijing Military Hospital Number 12, which was the name on the outside of the Black Prison, contained no meaningful medical facilities. Once inside, Moretti would never leave that building alive, although it would be said that he had received excellent care while at the prison.

Thanks to the creativity of the prison director, a plausible story had been formulated to explain Moretti's death. The coroner's report would give the cause of his death as an ingestion of tetrodotoxin originating from the ingestion of an improperly cleaned puffer fish at a restaurant before his arrest. Tetrodotoxin is 1,200 times more poisonous than cyanide. To substantiate the story, several other people would also be confirmed to have died from ingesting the deadly toxin at the same restaurant where Moretti and Han Li would supposedly have eaten.

It was well documented that deaths occur in China each year from people who eat the exotic fish at restaurants that fail to properly prepare the deadly fish. This would also make it possible to turn over Moretti's body without fear of contradicting the coroner's published cause of death. Ren Shi wasn't entirely sure whether the Americans would believe this story, but there was little they could do. Han Li, on the other hand, would be executed.

Ren Shi poured himself a cup of tea and considered the dedicated lieutenant colonel whom he'd sent to arrest the two thorns in his side and transport them to the prison. Unfortunately, that career army officer, along with the four soldiers who accompanied him to the Black Prison, would also have to be killed.

CHAPTER

11

The prison director was nervously pacing the well-worn carpet in his office, awaiting the arrival of two people whom he'd been told to expect almost three hours earlier. Ren Shi had called him early that morning and told him approximately what time the prisoners would arrive. The director was sure that he hadn't misunderstood, because he'd written down the time.

He debated whether to phone Ren Shi or continue to wait. After all, his responsibilities didn't begin until the prisoners arrived. Still, if anything went wrong, there was no telling whose head would be on the chopping block. Experience had taught him how things worked when one dealt with senior government officials. That thought tipped the scale, and he decided to call the Acting President of China.

As it turned out, getting hold of Ren Shi was easier said than done because the director had neglected to ask for his cell phone number when they had spoken that morning. He was forced to use the public number for Zhongnanhai, China's equivalent of the White House, but no matter how many times he called, he couldn't get past the operators. No one had any interest in taking even a "Please call me" message from a purported hospital administrator, much less connecting him to the most powerful person in the country ... or even that person's assistant.

Frustrated, the prison director eventually came up with a

plan. The next time he phoned, he told the operator that he had the results of the acting president's medical tests and that he needed to speak with Ren Shi immediately. The director gave his name and phone number, which the operator took down without hesitation. An hour later, his phone rang.

When the director informed Ren Shi that neither the prisoners nor their security detail had yet arrived, the phone went quiet for a full thirty seconds. Then he was told that their previous conversation had never happened—and the line went dead. The director didn't ask why Ren Si had changed his mind. Experience had taught him that knowing too much could sometimes be fatal, and he wondered if he too was going to have to worry about ingesting a bad preparation of puffer fish.

Bonaquist looked across the room at Yan He, who was lying unconscious on his bed and breathing normally. Earlier he'd removed the battery from the lieutenant colonel's cell phone and told the other agent to do the same with any phones found on the four soldiers whom he was looking after. If he couldn't get at the batteries, Bonaquist instructed the agent, he was to destroy the phones. No sense making it easy for the military to locate their men. He knew eventually they'd be found. China's electronic tracking technology was basically on par with that of most Western countries. Sooner or later, one of their geeks would figure out that Yan He and his men's cell phone signals last came from the vicinity of the St. Regis, where they'd been sent to arrest Moretti and Han Li. With that determination, the Chinese military would search the hotel from top to bottom.

The situation was further complicated by the fact that Bonaquist couldn't keep the lieutenant colonel and his men unconscious for much longer, because his supply of the sedative was almost depleted. When Yan He awoke, Bonaquist would have a lot of explaining to do, not that he expected it to do any good. He'd probably be arrested and tried by the Chinese government for kidnapping and assaulting the lieutenant colonel and his men. Even if a deal was struck and he didn't get jail time, he was out of the Secret Service. If he was lucky, he'd just be forced into retirement. If not, he'd do jail time for a host of federal charges, followed by a loss of pension and benefits.

This should have depressed Bonaquist, and yet he believed that he'd done the right thing. Neither the Chinese government nor the US government was making a lick of progress in their search for the presidents. Call it luck, instinct, or whatever you liked, but Moretti and Han Li had an innate ability to ferret things out. It was strange to think that with the vast number of government agencies on both sides of the world committed to this search, the presidents' best hope rested with a Chinese assassin and a medically discharged ex-alcoholic Army Ranger.

One mile before reaching the Inner Mongolian border, according to the road marker, Moretti asked Han Li to pull the car to the side of the road. He thought about putting the battery back in one of their phones to bring up a digital map of the area, but he knew full well that turning on either phone would give away their location. The Chinese government already knew Han Li's number. They probably also had Moretti's because the hotel's registration form had asked for it, and he'd foolishly written it down. He was sure that information had been entered into a government database shortly thereafter.

After leaving Bonaquist at the hotel, Moretti and Han Li had stopped at the twenty-four-hour Kinko's store they'd seen the previous day on their way to the mountain pass. Using Kinko's internet connection, they had searched for Sovereign Industries holdings in Inner Mongolia and found listings for three mines— but no addresses. On a Kinko's computer, Moretti had brought up MapQuest and zoomed in where the highway from Beijing crossed the Inner Mongolian border.

"A mine in Inner Mongolia would be the perfect place to hide the presidents," Moretti had said. "Who would think to look there? Since the pins in Wang's map seem to indicate that the mines were close to the border, let's see what we have." Scrolling the mouse across the computer screen, he had followed the main highway into Inner Mongolia. There appeared to be only one side road, which ran parallel and to the west of the main highway. Moretti and Han Li had agreed to begin their search for the mines there.

Sitting in their car a mile from the border, Han Li said, "We've got only six hours before the scheduled execution, so time is short. But we can't just drive up to the border crossing, because the military, and possibly other parts of the government, will be looking for us."

"You won't get an argument from me," agreed Moretti. "Our only option seems to be to go inland and drive across the pastureland until we're well past the border. We can then try to find the side road. If we're right, the mines will be along it."

"That path might be a good place to start," Han Li said, "but I don't know how far inland it goes." She pointed a hundred yards ahead and to her left, to a narrow pathway covered with crushed rock extending west into the grassland.

"Let's find out," Moretti replied, shifting the Audi into drive.

They started up the path, which went west for less than half a mile before it gradually turned northwest. Bisecting thousands of acres of tall undulating grass as they drove, the path began to slope upward until they reached the crest of a hill, where Moretti stopped the car. The unobstructed view ahead of them revealed only a sea of pastureland scarred by a line of wind turbines on a distant hill, where the path they were on ended.

"I think it's time to head straight north," said Moretti. "We should be far enough away from the highway so that no one will see or hear us. After two or three miles, we'll turn east and try to find the road we saw on MapQuest."

"I wonder what's beneath this grass," Han Li said as the Audi started off the path and nosed into the three-foot-high growth.

As it turned out, a great many hazards hid beneath the sea of green, all of which took a toll on the low-slung suburban automobile. A continuous series of ruts tested the durability of the Audi's German suspension system, while numerous rocks pinged off the undercarriage. Fortunately they were going slow enough to avoid most of the boulders and ditches, but they couldn't avoid them all. Those they encountered created sizable dents in both the driver and passenger doors and significantly loosened the front bumper.

Thirty minutes after leaving the path, they calculated, given their speed, that they were two to three miles into Inner Mongolia. Turning east, they soon intercepted the road that paralleled the main highway—a pothole-strewn, two-lane strip of dirt.

"Is this it?" Han Li asked as Moretti stopped the battered and bruised Audi.

"Yes, I think so. The heavy trucks and equipment needed for mining would tear up asphalt or concrete over time, but a hard-packed dirt road could easily be maintained. In any event, it's getting late." With that, Moretti put the pedal to the metal and they tore down the road, weaving to avoid potholes and looking for a mine that bore the Sovereign Industries logo.

Yan He slowly opened his eyes. Gradually gaining focus, he saw Bonaquist sitting in a chair beside his bed.

"Take it easy, Lieutenant Colonel. Have some water," Bonaquist said, steadying a glass for him.

The lieutenant colonel took a sip and slowly sat up. "Where am I?" he asked. As he tried to raise himself into a sitting position, he noticed the black-and-blue mark in the crook of his arm.

The Secret Service agent could tell that the lieutenant colonel knew what had happened. "You're in my hotel room, and you've been unconscious for almost seven hours."

"And my men?"

"They're still unconscious, but they'll be awake soon. I guess you've already figured out that you've been drugged. For the record, I alone made that call. Make sure you get that straight in your report."

"Why did you do it?" asked Yan He.

Bonaquist replied, "Despite what you might think, Moretti and Han Li are our only hope of finding and saving our presidents. We have just four hours before they're to be beheaded, and your help will be vitally important if what I think will happen actually does."

"You should explain," said Yan He.

So Bonaquist did.

Ren Shi was pacing back and forth in his office. How was he even going to find, much less kill, Moretti and Han Li? Their escape felt not unlike looking at a dam and watching a tiny crack slowly expand, powerless to stop its spread. Based on what he had learned about their investigative and analytical abilities, he assumed that they were on their way to Inner Mongolia. He didn't know how they'd find the presidents, but he didn't have a shred of doubt that they would. In his imagination, their deductive abilities had become almost supernatural.

So Ren Shi told Wang Lei to expect their arrival, and to make whatever preparations were necessary for the demise of these two particularly sharp thorns in his side. He also had their photos distributed to airports and train stations, as well as to Chinese and Inner Mongolian border guards. Maybe Han Li and Moretti would be stupid enough to try one of those means of entry, although Ren Shi seriously doubted it. With almost four hours left until the executions, he briefly considered accelerating the timetable, but then he quickly dismissed that notion. The beheadings would be streamed live and the time they would occur was well known. He didn't want to forfeit even a small percentage of the enormous audience who'd be watching.

Finally Ren Shi sat at his desk and removed a thirty-year-old Moutai from his bottom desk drawer, downing two shot glasses of the fiery liquid in rapid succession. His throat burned as the potent 120-proof liquor began to take effect and ease his anxieties. All he had to do was keep it together for 180 minutes. After that, he would be untouchable.

It was just past three o'clock in the afternoon. If the kidnappers stuck to their schedule, the presidents of China and the United States would be dead in slightly less than three hours. Moretti and Han Li had checked out three mining sites just off the dirt road, but none were owned by Sovereign Industries. Now approaching a fourth mine, they noted that it closely resembled the previous three. Each mine site had one or more rectangular corrugated-metal buildings behind which was an open pit or tunnel excavation, usually at some distance. In front of the three metal buildings at this mine site was a large steel sign with writing in Mongolian and Chinese. A smile broke on Moretti's face when he saw the Sovereign Industries logo.

"This is Wang Lei's coal mining subsidiary," Han Li said.

Getting out of the car, they observed a beehive of activity as large haulers, dump trucks, and other pieces of heavy equipment stripped coal from the pit mine.

"This doesn't look like a place where Wang Lei could hide the presidents," Han Li said. "Too many people around."

"No argument from me. Let's try the next mine," said Moretti, obviously disappointed. As they drove off, he noticed in the distance the line of white wind turbines they'd seen earlier. The irony of the old and new forms of energy, dirty and clean, side by side, struck him as ironic.

The next Sovereign Industries mine turned out to be four miles away. Again there were three corrugated-metal buildings and a sign that identified the site as Sovereign's copper mining subsidiary. Like the coal mine, it was a beehive of activity—and again Moretti and Han Li agreed that hiding hostages here would not have gone unnoticed.

As they continued down the dirt road, expecting to find the third mine within the next few miles, Moretti told Han Li to pull to the side of the road. When she stopped, he turned in his seat to face her. "If we're right about this, the presidents are at the third mine. And this close to the time of their execution, you can bet they'll have heavy security, especially along this road. Just one man with a .50-caliber machine gun could shred us and the car before we knew what was happening. At least, that's what I'd do if I was them."

"You're saying we should go off road again?" asked Han Li.

"Yes, we'll have a better chance of remaining unseen if we approach the mine from the tall grass."

As Han Li looked to her left, Moretti followed her gaze. The landscape seemed even more foreboding than their earlier off-road encounter. "I'm not sure we can get across that terrain without breaking an axle, tearing a tire, or worse," she said, pointing out several boulders that were almost completely hidden. "If anything happens to this car, we won't get to the mine in time. I think we should take this road a mile or two farther before we turn inland. It'll save us time."

"Or get us killed," said Moretti, "if they're waiting for us just ahead."

"A distinct possibility," Han Li agreed.

Moretti got out of the car and opened the trunk. Then he took out a pair of binoculars, two QBU-88 sniper rifles with suppressors, two Norinco Type 92 semi-automatic handguns, and two boxes of ammunition for each weapon. He gave Han Li a handgun, put the binoculars around his neck, and placed the rest of the arms and ammo between them. "Locked and loaded," he said. And with that, he sped up the dirt road.

Three hours before their scheduled execution, both presidents were moved to the building where they were to die. Once they left their cell, Kundek and his men removed the cell bars, cots, and everything else inside and carried it all to the smelter, which was two football fields west of them. At 2,200 degrees Fahrenheit, everything quickly liquefied or burned. The building was then scrubbed from floor to ceiling with bleach to eliminate any trace DNA. After the beheadings, they'd similarly clean the structure in which the executions occurred.

The presidents' bodies would be burned in the smelter, just as those of the four ministers previously killed had been. Then the ash residue would be taken a hundred miles away to a remote pasture and cast to the wind. Several loads of silver ore would be processed in the smelter to restore it to its normal appearance. Wang Lei had previously considered burying the bodies in a remote section of pastureland, but he had decided that would create an unacceptable risk if they were ever discovered. With three mines in the area, he could very easily become a suspect.

When Ren Shi called to tell him that Moretti and Han Li had escaped and were probably on their way to him, Wang Lei wasn't surprised. He didn't know how they could possibly discover where the presidents were imprisoned. But having witnessed their knack for uncovering the undiscoverable, he had little doubt that they'd be here. He ordered his men to set up an ambush a mile from the mine. They were to kill Moretti and Han Li on sight and without explanation.

Moretti continued down the dirt road for a little over a mile before turning west into the pastureland. Off road, the first half mile was strewn with large boulders effectively camouflaged by the tall grass. Even moving at no more than five miles an hour, the already dented Audi looked like it'd been the center of attention in a demolition derby. The terrain remained akin to a tank proving ground until they turned north, whereupon the boulders gradually decreased in size and number.

As the land began to level, Moretti took advantage of the situation and increased their speed to twenty miles an hour, even though the grass was getting noticeably higher. Eventually, when he was no longer able to see past the hood of the car or maintain a sense of direction, he took his foot off the gas. Five feet later, the car plunged nose first into an eight-foot-deep fissure, triggering the deployment of the driver and passenger airbags.

"Are you okay?" Moretti asked, pushing aside the deflated nylon bag connected to the steering wheel and unbuckling his seat belt.

Han Li assured him, "I'm fine."

The walls of the fissure into which Moretti had driven were two feet beyond the passenger side of the vehicle and three from the driver's side. But when he tried to open his door, it wouldn't budge. Han Li had a similar lack of success.

"I think the frame is twisted," Moretti said. He turned and looked up at the rear window, through which sunlight was entering the car. "The back end of the vehicle appears to be above the surface, so that's our way out," he said. He reached up and got a handhold, but as he lifted his right leg to climb on top of the driver's seat, a stabbing pain shot through his lower back and he let go.

Han Li saw what had happened and told Moretti that she had it. Grabbing the headrest, she effortlessly lifted herself onto the back of the passenger seat and side-kicked the rear window, instantly shattering it.

Moretti protected his face from the falling glass, and then brushed a dozen pieces from his hair and neck. When he looked up, Han Li was extending her arm down to him.

"Grab it," she said, helping him up to the back of the driver's seat and then out of the car. Then she made several trips back to retrieve their weapons and ammunition before joining him on the surface.

"Thanks for the help," Moretti said, sounding embarrassed. Then he handed her the binoculars and quickly changed the subject. "I don't see any patrols, not that they'd be all that visible in this tall grass."

Raising the binoculars and looking at the terrain north of them, Han Li agreed. Then she handed the binoculars back to Moretti and asked, "Any idea how far we are from the mine?"

"Not really. If we go with our original assumption, that the mines are three to four miles apart, then I'd say we're one to two miles away. But I'm just guessing."

"Then we'd better get moving," Han Li said. She slung the sniper rifle over her right shoulder, placed the handgun in the small of her back, and put as much ammo as she could carry in her pockets. Moretti did the same.

Navigating by the sun, they entered the tall grass in single file with Han Li taking the lead. Moretti's back was still bothering him, but he gritted his teeth and ignored the spasms and knifelike pain that punctuated every step as he matched the athletic Han Li stride for stride.

An hour and a half before the scheduled beheading, they came to the top of a hill. Taking out his binoculars and scanning the valley before them, Moretti immediately spotted a pit mine not far from where they were. Unlike the others they'd passed, this one was devoid of activity, and he couldn't tell whether it belonged to Wang Lei. However, the three corrugated-steel buildings at this site appeared identical to those at the two other mines. Although he didn't see any patrols, Moretti suspected that the white pickup trucks in front of one of the buildings were for that purpose.

Fifteen minutes later they'd worked their way to the front of the buildings, where the frontage sign indicated that this was Sovereign Industries' silver mining subsidiary.

"Two parked trucks. Hardly the security I expected," Han Li said, pointing to the vehicles.

"On the other hand, this could be exactly the outward appearance they want," said Moretti. "At a mine that appears to be inactive, too many vehicles or security personnel would raise questions. Let's check the buildings. For all we know, the presidents are within or beneath them."

They started their search with the building where the security vehicles were parked. When Han Li tried the front doorknob, it turned in her hand. She nodded to her partner and threw the door open. The four uniformed security guards, who were sitting around a square wooden table playing mah-jongg, raised their hands in stunned silence when they saw the two silenced rifles pointed directly at them.

"I don't know what they're guarding, but I can tell you it's not the presidents," Moretti said, after frisking them and not finding so much as a handgun or knife.

"Let me see what I can find out." Han Li grabbed one of the men and roughly shoved him out the front door. Five minutes later she returned with the guard. "These men are here to keep away squatters and those who want to prospect on the property. Normally only two guards are on duty, but there's a shift change at six and the other two came in early to play mah-jongg. All four guards live in the workers' dormitory at the copper mine."

"Anything else?" asked Moretti.

"He says the other two buildings are empty. Guard them while I look." Ten minutes later, Han Li returned. The buildings were empty.

An hour before the scheduled beheadings, Moretti knew they were at a dead end and out of clues.

China's minister of defense was briefing Ren Shi on the scheduled airstrikes against the African strongholds of the Protectors of Islam. Weapons release would begin at 6:30 p.m. Beijing time, unless there was proof that the presidents were still alive. The exact geographical coordinates for these strongholds had been provided by the Americans, which Ren Shi couldn't have imagined happening just a few months earlier.

The airborne assault would be conducted by H-6K bombers, the equivalent of America's B-52s. Each would carry up to six CJ-10A cruise missiles secured to its four underwing pylons. The aircraft were fueled and the crews ready for takeoff at military bases in Ethiopia, Zimbabwe, Malawi, Gambia, and Zambia. The minister of defense pointed out that although there were substantially fewer strongholds for this terrorist group in Africa than in the Middle East, unfortunately they were spread throughout ten countries. China therefore had to launch its aircraft almost forty-five minutes before e-hour to adhere to the attack plan they had coordinated with the Americans. If they were late, the terrorists within the strongholds would find out about the American attack and scatter. American aircraft were already airborne. The minister of defense asked for permission to launch the aircraft at e-hour minus forty-five minutes, and Ren Shi agreed without hesitation.

General Ronald Trowbridge was sitting in the Pentagon's operations center and looking at six large screens. Displayed before him was a detailed map of the Middle East that indicated the air force's and navy's weapons platforms and, after launch, the flight tracks of the cruise missiles on the way to their targets.

For this mission, the navy's ordnance of choice was the Tomahawk, a long-range subsonic cruise missile weighing a ton and a half, and slightly over 18 feet in length and 20.4 inches in diameter. Traveling at 550 mph, it carried a lethal payload of one thousand pounds of high explosive. Anyone unfortunate enough to be within ninety feet of where it hit would be killed instantly, and most structures within that kill zone would be destroyed. Anyone within 650 feet of impact would be either killed or wounded. Two Ohio-class ballistic missile submarines, which had been previously converted to launch the Tomahawk, were off the coast of Pakistan and counting down to e-hour.

The United States Air Force, which would launch the bulk of the firepower for this assault, sent ten B-52H Stratofortress bombers to take out its targets. Each aircraft carried six air-to-ground missiles on external pylons, along with eight on an internal rotary launcher. They were currently over the Arabian Sea.

Nine of the ten aircraft carried a combination of AGM-86C and -86D model air-to-ground cruise missiles. Each was nearly 21 feet in length, 24.5 inches in diameter, weighed a ton and a half, and carried a three-thousand-pound explosive payload, three times that of the Tomahawk. Each model was designed to address a specific type of target. The AGM-86C had a blast fragmentation warhead that broke into predictably sized pieces that traveled at high velocity and caused a tremendous amount of damage to surface targets on impact. The AGM-86D, in contrast, carried a penetration warhead that went deep into a hardened or submerged target before detonating. The tenth aircraft carried twenty AGM-86Ds and was being sent to a well-known hiding place for terrorists within a particularly rugged mountain range in northwest Pakistan.

CHAPTER

12

H an Li walked outside and told Moretti that she'd just bound and gagged the security guards, but he didn't hear a word she was saying. He was staring, as if in a trance, at the open pit mine in the distance.

"Where's that light coming from?" he finally asked.

"What light?" asked Han Li, looking in the direction he was staring.

"Straight ahead of you."

Han Li looked again, but still didn't see anything.

Moretti pointed and said, "Draw an imaginary line from my finger to the back of the pit, then look two inches above the ground. There's a tiny sliver of light."

Following his instructions, Han Li spotted what he was looking at. "How were you able to see that?" she asked.

"I have 20/15 vision," explained Moretti. "You seem to have a good relationship with one of the guards. Why don't you ask him where that light is coming from?"

Han Li went back into the building and grabbed the same person she'd questioned earlier. Hauling him outside, she removed his gag, pointed to what Moretti was looking at, and asked him what it was. Apparently fearing what would happen if he didn't cooperate, the guard quickly answered her.

Han Li told Moretti, "He says the light comes on automatically each day, and that it's from one of the buildings on the other side of the pit."

"What buildings? Moretti raised his binoculars and looked again. Because of the tall grass, however, he couldn't see any structures—just the light.

Han Li questioned the guard further. "He swears that the buildings are there. Also that the other side of the pit has its own security force. He and the other guards sometimes encounter them on the gravel path that circumvents the mine. They have strict instructions not to go near those buildings."

A few questions later, it was apparent that the man knew little else. Han Li replaced his gag and led him back inside the building.

Upon returning, she asked Moretti, "Do you think the presidents are in one of those buildings?"

"With the beheadings less than an hour away, that's what I want to believe."

Moretti and Han Li kept low, crouching in the high grass as they made their way toward the light. A third of the way there, they saw two guards at the edge of a gravel roadway that bordered the grass. Neither guard felt the impact of the heavy rounds that entered their skulls.

Dragging the two bodies into the grass, Han Li and Moretti continued toward the two buildings, which were now visible. Several minutes later, they noticed a white pickup traveling toward them. The truck was high enough so that the driver could see not only them, but also the two dead bodies. As if on cue, the vehicle come to a screeching halt directly adjacent to the men they'd killed.

Han Li's shot went through the front windshield of the pickup and into the guard's forehead before he could raise the microphone to his mouth.

While Moretti dragged the two dead guards out of the grass and into the bed of the pickup, Han Li did the same with the dead driver from the front seat. The bullet hadn't shattered the windshield, but it did create a large hole with multiple cracks emanating from it. Moretti got behind the wheel and pulled the pickup into a small cluster of trees eight hundred yards from the buildings.

Looking through his binoculars, he saw four guards standing post in front of the entry door to one of the structures. "I see four guards. The presidents have to be inside that structure."

"That's what I was thinking," said Han Li. "But we can't drive there in this vehicle. That bullet hole in the windshield might as well be a neon sign."

"With only twenty-five minutes before the scheduled execution, we haven't got a choice," Moretti said. "This truck will at least be familiar to the guards when they see it approach. Let's see if we can park behind one of those buildings before anyone notices that we're not guards."

Han Li agreed. "Like you said, we haven't got a choice."

No sooner had they pulled back onto the gravel road than they saw a black SUV headed in their direction. "Go over that small hill," Han Li said, pointing to their right.

Moretti did as he was told. When they crested the hill, they quickly abandoned the security vehicle and hid in the deep grass. A few seconds later the SUV pulled up behind the pickup truck. Four men, dressed in the same black pants and long-sleeved black shirts as the men they'd killed earlier, got out of the SUV and headed for the pickup. This time Moretti shot first, dropping two guards in rapid succession. Han Li was a split second behind. She drilled the first guard between the eyes, and her second shot found the right temple of the other.

They placed the four bodies in the back of the pickup, on top of the other three. Leaving the pickup truck where it was, they got in the SUV. As they drove, they saw the huge Mongolian, who less than a day earlier had tried to kill them, entering the heavily guarded building. It was now 5:40 p.m.

Moretti drove the SUV to the rear of the building that the

Mongolian had entered. No one gave their vehicle a second glance; the SUV was a patrol vehicle and the heavily tinted windows prevented them from being seen. Moretti initially thought that he and Han Li would quietly kill the four guards in front of the building and then take anyone inside by surprise, but he knew that plan was risky. People don't always die quietly, and if those inside thought they were being attacked, the presidents would probably be killed on the spot. Assuming they *were* inside, of course, which Moretti believed to be the case.

As they drove the SUV behind the structure, and Moretti saw that the generator was operating, a better idea came to him. He told Han Li what he was thinking and then got out of the SUV, walked over to the generator, and turned it off. Then he continued to lean over the now silent and powerless electrical supply for the building until he heard someone coming up behind him.

Turning around, Moretti saw a guard—five foot eight with closely cropped black hair and a thick torso—pointing an AK-47 at the center of his chest. The look on the man's face wasn't that of someone who intended to take a prisoner. Instead, it was the glint of satisfaction that a hunter experiences when he knows he's cornered his prey. However, an instant later that expression changed to one of astonishment as a two-inch hole appeared on the left side of the guard's chest and he crumpled lifeless to the ground.

When Moretti turned to join Han Li, he saw a man slowly approaching her from behind. Apparently she'd been so consumed with her shot that she hadn't heard him. Except for being bald, he looked much like the guard Han Li had just killed—roughly the same height and build. Twenty feet away, he slowly began to level his gun at the back of her head.

Relying on muscle memory from his days with the Rangers, in one smooth motion Moretti removed the knife from the scabbard beneath his belt and threw it with all the strength he had. The blade missed Han Li by less than six inches, flying by her with such speed that she didn't have time to react. Completely focused on his kill shot, the terrorist never knew what happened. One minute he was aiming at his victim, and the next it was lights out. The blade had buried itself to the hilt in the man's chest and cleaved his heart.

Han Li was still staring at the dead man when Moretti retrieved his weapon, cleaning the blade on the man's shirt before returning it to his scabbard. "Where'd you get the knife?" she asked.

"From Gao Hui's armory in the Audi. I'm thinking that in less than a minute, someone misses these two and comes looking for them."

"Which means," said Han Li, "that we need to start killing people before then."

Wang Lei wondered what was taking the guards so long. He needed them to hurry and get the generator back on line because time was running short. The presidents had been sedated and were quietly kneeling in front of the Protectors of Islam flag. Delaying their deaths was unthinkable to Wang Lei. The beheadings must be streamed live, and the consequences of failing to broadcast on time would be catastrophic. In order for the attacks to occur, the world had to see the presidents die.

Since the building had no windows and—at the moment— no electricity, the only light came from two small battery-powered lanterns. That was a far cry from the powerful tungsten-halogen lamps that were fastened to a ceiling grid high above Wang Lei. He looked at his watch and decided that he couldn't afford to waste time. Even if they managed to get the generator back on line, there was no guarantee that it would function properly during the broadcast. He turned to Kundek and told him to move the executions outside as quickly as possible, while there was still daylight. The presidents needed to be dead in twenty minutes, and Wang Lei was going to make sure that happened.

At thirty-five minutes to e-hour, the Chinese and American flight crews had completed their prelaunch checklists and were waiting for their timers to tick down to zero before releasing their ordnance. Using satellite GPS data to navigate, each cruise missile would remain at high altitude until it reached a predetermined geographical point, at which time it would descend and continue its journey within a few meters of the earth to avoid detection by radar.

The two Ohio-class submarines, traveling one hundred feet below the surface and using compressed air to expel their cruise missiles from vertical tubes, would launch their ordnance toward predetermined targets at the same time. Like the air force's AGM and the Chinese CJ-10K cruise missiles, each weapon would be guided by a GPS chip that received instructions from an orbiting satellite. Just like their air force and Chinese counterparts, the crews of both submarines were ready to launch.

Moretti and Han Li took position on opposite sides of the building. On the razor's edge of time, their plan was simple and direct. First they would kill the two remaining guards in front of the door, and then they'd enter and shoot the bad guys before they could harm the presidents. Peering around their respective corners of the building, Moretti and Han Li each took aim at the guard closest to them. When Moretti held up five fingers, Han Li understood and began her silent countdown. Just as they reached four, however, the front door burst open and they quickly withdrew their rifles.

Wang Lei and President Liu were the first to emerge. The industrialist was carrying a laptop computer under his left arm, and he had a cell phone in his left hand and a handgun in his right. They were followed by Kundek, who was escorting President Ballinger. Five guards, each carrying an AK-47, were the last to leave the building. One guard, who had a Protectors of Islam flag draped around his neck, also carried a camera and tripod. Two other guards held long knives and were wearing balaclavas.

Moretti considered picking off the terrorists, knowing that Han Li would follow his lead, but he quickly changed his mind and removed his finger from the trigger. The group had spread out as they emerged from the building, which meant that he and Han Li would need more time to line up their shots. That would give the terrorists an opportunity to fire one or more rounds at the presidents. Although he didn't like it, Moretti decided that waiting until everyone was grouped together for the execution was the safer choice. Han Li apparently agreed because he saw her also remove her finger from the trigger.

Wang Lei directed the group to a small patch of grass on which the late-afternoon sun continued to shine. Then he shoved President Liu toward Kundek, who grabbed him by the shoulder. Now with a president in each huge hand, the Mongolian forced the two men to their knees. Coming out from under the influence of the sedative, the presidents tried to resist, but they had no chance against Kundek's strength and weight.

When the guard finished connecting the cable between his camera and Wang Lei's laptop, he handed the flag to the man beside him and told Wang Lei that he had good video, but no internet connection. Wang Lei cursed and told him to get on with it because it would be dark soon, after which the guard announced loudly that he was now filming. The two terrorists wearing balaclavas took position behind the presidents, grabbed their hair, pulled their heads back, and placed their knives against the presidents' throats. Just as Moretti and Han Li were taking aim at the executioners, the guard holding the flag handed one end to the man next to him. As they stretched the flag taut behind the presidents, it blocked Moretti and Han Li's view.

The ex–Army Ranger decided that it was now or never. In rapid succession, he put bullets through the heads of the guards holding the flag. As the two dead guards dropped the flag, the presidents and their would-be executioners were again visible. Han Li unleashed two rounds, one into the left hemisphere of the brain of each executioner, preventing any movement of their arms before they collapsed lifeless to the ground.

As soon as he saw people around him being shot, the camera operator started to run. In doing so, he dropped the camera and inadvertently ripped out the cable connecting it to the computer. Since she didn't have a shot at Wang Lei, who had taken refuge behind the tree to his right, Han Li's third bullet went into the skull of the camera operator.

The next rounds all came from Kundek firing his AK-47 on full auto at Han Li and Moretti, who dove to the ground and barely avoided the volley of bullets. While they were pinned down by rounds from a second magazine that the Mongolian quickly jammed into his weapon, Wang Lei retrieved the camera, computer, and phone, and then ran to a nearby SUV. As Kundek continued reloading and firing, the industrialist pulled alongside him just long enough for the Mongolian to jump into the vehicle, and they raced down the gravel path toward the dirt road.

Moretti and Han Li ran to the two presidents, who were still lying on the ground. Both men were unharmed and almost free of the sedative's influence.

"Did the cavalry arrive?" Ballinger asked.

Moretti looked at Han Li, who was speaking with President Liu and helping him stand, before he answered. "No, Mr. President, it's just Han Li and me. We need to get you both out of here before Wang Lei regroups and comes back with reinforcements. Are you all right to walk?"

"Let's just get moving," said Ballinger. "I'm not sticking around for that psychopath to return."

Retrieving the black SUV that they'd parked behind the building, Moretti and Han Li helped the presidents into the backseat and strapped them in. Moretti took the wheel and headed south across the grassland, electing to avoid the dirt road where he believed that Wang Lei and his men would be waiting in ambush.

The problem with their route, however, was that it was slow.

The tall grass hid fissures like the one they'd driven into earlier, so Moretti had to drive at a snail's pace. After the sun set, they minimized their visibility as much as possible by using only the vehicle's running lights, which slowed them down even more. As Moretti wove his way around numerous obstacles and careened off those he didn't see, the SUV suddenly sputtered, lurched forward, and stopped.

Moretti stared in frustration at the red light that appeared on his indicator panel and exclaimed, "Could this day get any more perfect?" They were out of gas.

Taking the cell phone from his pocket and reinserting the battery, Moretti found Bonaquist's card and dialed the Secret Service agent's cell. He figured that Wang Lei already had a good idea of where they were, so it really didn't matter whether the industrialist's friends in the government could triangulate Moretti's position.

What Moretti needed now was help, but he quickly realized that help was not an option. His call to Bonaquist wasn't being answered. Moretti looked at his cell phone and saw that not a single bar appeared on his screen. With no food, water, vehicle, or cellular service, his optimism that they'd escape was fast evaporating. In six short hours, daylight would return—and Moretti had no doubt that at sunrise, the Chinese industrialist would come after him with everything he had.

Wang Lei drove straight to the roadblock, a mile down the road from where he'd hidden the hostages. Earlier he'd told the five men stationed there that two extremely dangerous convicts had escaped from prison, and that they'd murdered one of his employees and stolen a car. Then he had given them descriptions of Moretti and Han Li. The Mongolian tribal mind-set was that anyone who committed such crimes should not be tried, but instead should suffer the same fate as their victims. So they had no problem with setting up a roadblock to catch—and kill—the two convicts.

Now Wang Lei directed those same five men to search the pastureland between the silver mine and the Chinese border for the convicts, whose number had increased from two to four. He suspected that the reason Moretti and Han Li had come across the grassland in the first place was that they suspected an ambush on the local road, and he had no reason to believe that assumption had changed. If he was in Moretti's position, he'd head south through the tall grass until he crossed into China, where recognition of the presidents by locals would assure their protection and safety.

After his men departed, Wang Li went to the copper mine and assembled his security staff. He ordered the eight guards on duty to pair up, two to a truck, and search the pastureland between the mine and the border. They would be looking for four people, who might be either walking or in a vehicle. Wang Li gave the eight guards the same background story that he'd given to the five men at the roadblock, again not revealing the identities of the four people for whom they were to search. Once the four people were spotted by either search party, he and Kundek would send the guards away and take care of the rest.

The reason Wang Lei was in this predicament was that everyone who had participated in the abductions was now dead, except Kundek. That wasn't necessarily bad news, because he had intended to eventually kill them all anyway. However, it did complicate the situation, since now he had no choice but to use his mining security team for the search. If one or more of them saw the presidents, then a few more names would have to make their way onto the casualty list.

When the guards left, Wang Lei watched the aborted video recording, cut the footage showing the deaths of the guards and executioners, and made a few other adjustments. The revised footage would show President Ballinger and President Liu kneeling with knives to their throats, before the flag of the Protectors of Islam. Then the screen would go black, followed by an announcement that they had been beheaded. Now all Wang Lei had to do was find them and make that happen.

At 6:00 p.m. Beijing time, Acting President Houck and the National Security Council were in the Situation Room, looking intently at one of the six computer screens positioned around them. Although the link that had been publicly released wasn't yet active, they expected that at any moment, the presidents would suffer the same grim fate as the other hostages. At 6:27 p.m. however, having still witnessed no evidence of the beheadings, Houck decided to call off the attack.

He was picking up the phone to inform Ren Shi of this, and then tell General Trowbridge to issue the abort code, when the terrorist's internet link suddenly became active, and a video appeared on the room's video monitors. Although it lasted just a few seconds and showed only the executioners with their knives to the throats of their two victims, an attached message announced that both leaders had been killed. Houck was convinced that President Ballinger and President Liu were dead. He wondered why, given the videos of the previous killings, the Protectors had been unwilling to show the beheadings, but he was grateful for it.

"Sir, we've reached e-hour," General Trowbridge said, breaking the silence that permeated the room.

CHAPTER

13

At 6:30 p.m. Beijing time, ten B-52Hs began launching what eventually would number two hundred AGM-86C and -86D cruise missiles. Once free of the aircraft, the $1.2 million airborne bombs accelerated to Mach 0.73, approximately 550 mph, and accepted pinpoint guidance from their coupled global positioning and initial navigation systems.

When the last of the missiles had dropped free of the giant bombers, each of the aircraft made a standard rate turn of fifteen degrees to starboard and set course for the seven KC-10 Extender aerial refueling tankers that were awaiting their arrival. The modified DC-10s would fuel each plane to its 312,000-pound capacity, enabling the gas-guzzling, eight-engine aircraft to begin their long journey back to the Second Bomb Wing at Barksdale AFB, Louisiana, half a world away.

As the B-52s dropped their payloads, the missile launch officers on board two Ohio Class submarines, the *Florida* and the *Ohio*, turned their keys in unison, each beginning the process of sending twenty-five of their 154 Tomahawk missiles to their targets. Afterward, both combat platforms would remain on station in case additional launches were required.

At the same time, China dropped a total of 120 CJ-10K cruise missiles, each with a maximum range of 1,200 miles, from twenty H-6K bombers that were scattered throughout the African continent. The airborne bombs, traveling at approximately the same speed as their American counterparts, crossed the borders of eleven African countries at treetop level, streaking toward the Protectors of Islam strongholds. At that moment, a total of 370 cruise missiles were traveling at just under the speed of sound to their assigned targets.

Awalmir Afridi, along with twenty of his closest followers, was hiding deep within his ancestral cave in the mountains of northwest Pakistan, awaiting the massive explosions that he knew would engulf the area around them. Even though he had no communication with the outside world, he assumed that the two presidents had been beheaded at the appointed time, and that the Americans and Chinese were going to blame him for their deaths. The United States, at least, was sure to send a military response that would offer a cataclysmic warning to anyone contemplating similar actions.

One thing in Afridi's favor was that no one knew exactly where he was hiding, but he knew that the United States would solve that problem by bombing the entire area. Even though he had more than a year's worth of supplies stored in the cave, along with an unlimited amount of clean water from deep within the earth, Afridi still worried. The expected onslaught of bombs would cause landslides in the ancient and fractured mountain, conceivably sealing all the cave's exits under tons of rock and debris.

Whoever was responsible for the kidnappings and executions had done an impeccable job of framing Afridi. By handing the Protectors to the United States and China on a silver platter, the guilty party could operate without fear of reprisal. Afridi didn't know who was behind this, but if he survived, he'd make it his life's work to extract his revenge.

Four hours before sunset, Afridi summoned everyone within the cave to Asr, afternoon prayer. Each person took a small rug from a stack in the corner and placed it on the ground so that it pointed in the direction of Mecca, Saudi Arabia. Twenty-one people were prostrated in prayer when the first AGM-86D cruise missile slammed into the mountain peak high above them. The shock wave that followed reverberated throughout the cave with such force that everyone and everything was tossed around like a rag doll in the hands of a child. A moment later, the cave was plunged into darkness.

The update that Ren Shi got from Wang Lei was not at all what he had expected. Instead of hearing that the two presidents, Moretti, and Han Li were all dead, Ren Shi was told that they'd escaped and were probably headed toward the Chinese border. He was terrified at the thought that President Liu might encounter someone who would recognize him and summon help. If that happened, the dominoes would begin to fall. Wang Lei would be named as the mastermind behind the kidnappings, after which the interrogators would squeeze from him the identities of everyone else involved.

Ren Shi briefly considered sending a special ops team to the copper mine to kill Wang Lei and his men, but that thought evaporated when he realized the mountain of circumstantial evidence that pointed his way. The rope that hung most heavily around Ren Shi's neck was that he had granted permission for Wang Lei to use a military transport helicopter because the helicopters owned by Sovereign Industries carried a maximum of four people. Even though the industrialist was an accomplished pilot, flew the aircraft by himself, and returned it seven hours later, there would still be questions about why he had needed a transport helicopter at that time of day, especially one that could carry two dozen people.

Ren Shi was convinced that the only way to get out of this alive was to make sure that none of the four—Moretti, Han Li, or either president—reached the border or got a chance to speak with anyone. Anything short of that … and Ren Shi's head was squarely on the chopping block.

Just as he picked up the phone to call the local airbase commander, his assistant entered the office to tell him that the White House was on the line. As it turned out, the Acting President of the United States was very talkative that evening.

The temperature in the pastureland, which had been shirtsleeve warm during the day, was dropping and would eventually fall to the high forties before morning. They had run out of gas near a hill, along which ran the row of giant wind turbines that Moretti and Han Li had seen earlier that day. The enormous machines would have been invisible in the darkness were it not for the flashing obstruction lights atop each turbine.

Leaning against the outside of the SUV, Moretti and Han Li looked at the presidents, who were asleep in the backseat.

"They're too exhausted to walk," Han Li said, turning off a battery-powered lantern she had found in the cargo compartment.

"When daylight comes," said Moretti, "it won't be hard for Wang Lei's men to follow our car tracks through the grass. And if they send search aircraft, we can't hide for long in the tall grass. We need to get over the border before then, and there's only one way to do that."

"Get another vehicle," Han Li said.

"You read my mind. I'm thinking that the copper mine is somewhere in that direction," Moretti said, pointing to his left. "We know there are vehicles there because we saw them when we passed by earlier today. I'll steal one and drive it back here."

"How will you find us? Eye navigating by Polaris doesn't exactly give you GPS accuracy," said Han Li said, referring to the North Star.

"Third light from the left," Moretti responded, pointing to the obstruction light atop one of the wind turbines.

"That works. But if you're not back in three hours, I'll have to wake the presidents. Tired or not, we'll need to get moving toward the border without you. Otherwise, as you said, Wang Lei's men won't have any trouble finding us."

"Do whatever you have to do to keep them safe." With that, Moretti got his bearings and stepped into the void of night.

Walking through the pastureland was more difficult than Moretti had anticipated. He had only starlight to help him avoid the holes, ditches, and fissures that permeated the area. Adopting a cautious pace to avoid spraining or even breaking an ankle or leg, he still came close a couple of times.

An hour after he'd left the SUV, Moretti heard the faint but unmistakable sound of a vehicle and saw a pair of approaching headlights no more than a hundred yards away. As he moved out of its path and waited for it to pass, he had a thought. Unslinging his rifle, he watched as the four-passenger pickup, going no more than five miles an hour, passed beside him. Trying to maintain control over the uneven terrain, the driver never saw the butt of Moretti's rifle smash through the side window and strike the side of his head. Nor did the security guard in the passenger seat, momentarily stunned by what happened, move in time to avoid the rifle butt that slammed into the center of his forehead.

When the truck coasted to a stop, Moretti pulled the driver out, placed the vehicle in park, and dragged the other guard out. He bound their wrists and legs with the plastic handcuffs he found in the rear cab and used their shirts to gag them. Then he got into the vehicle and pointed it at the third obstruction light from the left.

Twenty minutes later, Moretti reached the general area where he believed he had left the presidents and Han Li, whereupon he stopped and exited the vehicle. Gauging distance from a single light source isn't usually all that accurate, but he believed he was close. When he walked in front of the headlights so that he could be seen, he saw Han Li stand up in the tall grass where she was hiding and come toward him with a rifle in her hands.

"Thank you for not killing me," Moretti said, looking at the gun.

"It's a good thing you walked in front of the lights," explained Han Li, "because I didn't expect you back so soon. How'd you get the truck?"

"I persuaded two security guards to give it to me. How are the presidents doing?"

"Not well. I don't think they were given much to eat or drink while they were held hostage. They're hungry and thirsty, with very little energy. This cold temperature will make them ill if they stay outside much longer," Han Li said.

"Let's get them inside the pickup and turn up the heat," suggested Moretti. "The driver's window is broken, but there should still be enough warm air circulating to make them more comfortable."

Han Li guided Moretti back to the SUV, and they moved the presidents into the pickup's rear passenger compartment and fastened their seat belts. Moretti then turned up the heat as high as it would go and headed south across the pastureland.

They'd been driving no more than fifteen minutes when Moretti heard someone speaking in Chinese. The voice sounded as if it was coming from beneath him. He groped under the driver's seat, found a handheld radio, and gave it to Han Li.

"One of the drivers failed to check in, so they're now directing all vehicles to search this area," she interpreted for him.

"They know we're heading straight for China," said Moretti. "I hope that we have enough of a head start to beat them to the border."

"We will … unless Wang Lei sends a security team from his coal mine, which is only four miles ahead of us," Han Li added.

"Doesn't being a realist ever get tiring?" asked Moretti.

Han Li ignored the question.

The terrain was becoming somewhat smoother, so Moretti doubled his speed to ten miles per hour. As best as he could recall, it was approximately ten miles from the border to the copper mine. He felt the percentages were squarely on his side—until a low-flying aircraft passed directly overhead.

Moretti immediately turned off his lights and slowed down. Sticking his head through the opening where the side window had once been, he watched as the plane did a 180-degree turn and came back toward them, its powerful landing light illuminating the area in front of it. Moretti quickly veered the pickup to the left to get out of its path, but he was a split second too slow. The aircraft's landing light raked the back of the truck. Cautioning the presidents to tighten their seat belts and hold on, he turned the vehicle back to a southerly heading and increased speed.

"Since they're not shooting at us, it's probably just a reconnaissance aircraft. All they can do is report our location, so now it's just a footrace to the border," Moretti said to Han Li as they violently bounced across the terrain. He reached into his jacket pocket, pulled out his cell phone, and handed it to her. "Do me a favor and see if we have a signal."

Not a single bar showed on the screen. "Nothing," Han Li said, handing the phone back to Moretti.

"Maybe we'll have better luck closer to the border."

They again heard the aircraft approaching, and seconds later the pickup truck was raked by its light. This time, however, instead of turning around, the plane maintained a southerly heading until its lights faded in the distance.

"You were right about the vehicles from the coal mine," Moretti said to Han Li, who didn't need to ask what he meant. In front of them, two lines of vehicles were converging on their position, moving in opposing arcs approximately a mile apart.

"There's no way for us to get around them as long as we're driving on this obstacle course," Moretti said. "They'll just surround us and then fire every weapon they have at us."

"Unless …," said Han Li.

"Unless what?"

"Stop the truck and let me out," she said. "Then follow me."

Moretti did as he was told and brought the pickup to a halt. He then stayed close to Han Li as she sprinted ahead, apparently unaffected by the dark and uneven terrain. When they'd gone a little more than three hundred yards, she held up her arm to indicate that he should stop the truck. Moretti got out of the pickup and joined her, followed by the two presidents. Looking at the converging arcs, Moretti estimated that the vehicles were no more than five to six minutes away.

"I'm guessing that you two have a plan," President Ballinger said hopefully, as he looked at the huge black hole in front of them.

"I do, but we have to act quickly if it's going to work," replied Han Li, who then explained what she was going to do.

As Han Li steered, Moretti pushed. The pickup moved slowly at first, and then gained momentum as it encountered the downward slope toward the coal pit. Once the front tires cleared the ledge, the truck nosed over and plummeted several hundred feet, hitting the service road that spiraled to the bottom of the pit and rolling over to continue its journey to the floor of the mine, where it burst into flames. The crash and the eventual explosion could be heard for miles.

As the car accelerated toward the bottom of the pit, Moretti and Han Li took the presidents back to the tall grass, less than fifty yards away, and found a large ditch where they could all hide. Then they waited.

When the two arcs of vehicles converged, Wang Lei and Kundek got out of their vehicle and looked into the pit. Both knew there was no way anyone could survive such a crash. Moments later the vehicles departed, and the area was again immersed in darkness.

"Well done," President Liu said to Moretti and Han Li.

"I couldn't agree more," said President Ballinger.

"They'll come back in the morning to retrieve our bodies from the pit," Moretti said.

"Which brings up the question," added Ballinger, "of how we get to the border before daylight without a vehicle."

"That, Mr. President, is a very good question," Moretti replied.

Ren Shi was ecstatic upon learning that Moretti, Han Li, and the two presidents were dead. He gave himself all the credit for what had happened. If he hadn't sent a military training aircraft to search the area, Wang Lei would never have found them, nor would they have driven to their deaths while trying to avoid capture.

Now that this mess was behind him, he could finally go on CCTV and solemnly report to the Chinese people that both President Liu and President Ballinger had been beheaded by the Protectors of Islam, and that their bodies had been burned and mutilated beyond recognition after their executions. That last part should increase everyone's blood pressure, he thought, as he fine-tuned his speech. He'd just have to make sure that whatever remains of President Ballinger he returned to the United States was mostly tissue, so that they'd be unable to determine the actual cause of death.

In the same speech, Ren Shi would announce that China and the United States had jointly taken military action to annihilate the radical Islamic group responsible for this heinous crime. Ren Shi knew that appearance was everything in Chinese politics. His working alongside the United States, and being statesmanlike in explaining to the people the retaliatory actions that were being jointly undertaken, would all but ensure that the Party would name him as the next president of China.

CHAPTER

14

Although it seemed like an eternity, the barrage of cruise missiles that hit the mountainous area surrounding Afridi's cave lasted only five minutes. When the assault ended, the founder of the Protectors of Islam began coughing uncontrollably. He took out the flashlight he carried in his pants pocket, turned it on, and picked himself up off the dirt floor. Dazed and unsteady, he had difficulty breathing, and what little air he was getting into his lungs between coughing fits felt like sandpaper. Shining his light around him, he saw that the air was thick with fine brown particles of rock dust shaken free from the upper reaches of the cave.

When Afridi's coughing subsided, he dusted himself off as best he could and made his way to the front of the cave to check the main entrance. Given the severity of the attack, he was worried that any or all of six openings to the cave might have become blocked by falling debris. When he arrived at what should have been a large gaping hole to the outside, he felt his knees buckle. A pile of rocks extended ten feet into the cave. This greatly concerned him because the main entrance was the best protected of the six openings to the outside. Throughout the centuries, a sloping ledge above this opening had always deflected rocks and debris away from the cave.

Panicked that the remaining portals, which were spread over

the length of six football fields, might have suffered a similar fate, he went to check. Thirty minutes later, exhausted and still having difficulty breathing because of the particulate matter that remained in his lungs, Afridi sat down on a large boulder and ran his coarse hands over his dusty face.

Every exit to the outside was blocked, something that Afridi would not have believed possible less than an hour earlier. He pictured himself slowly suffocating, entombed in this dark and airless hole. No, he had to get a grip on the situation and figure out how to escape. The obvious challenge was how to remove tons of debris from one of the openings, letting air into the cave before the carbon dioxide rose to a lethal level.

Afridi discounted the option of concentrating everyone's efforts on excavating one portal. If the debris covering the chosen portal was too thick or unmovable boulders were in the way, they'd waste valuable time and air. The best approach was to find where the landslide of rocks was the thinnest within the six blocked portals, and then concentrate their manpower there. Energized that he had the semblance of a plan, even though it was razor thin and fragile, Afridi went to organize his men.

The temperature was rapidly dropping, and both presidents were shivering. Moretti guessed that they were between five and six miles from the border. Because of the uneven terrain and the presidents' mental and physical exhaustion, walking there would take six hours, perhaps longer. Unfortunately it would be daylight long before then. Taking a good look at the wreckage in the pit, Wang Lei would notice a distinct lack of corpses. After that, the industrialist would concentrate his land and airborne surveillance between the border and the pit. When he did, they were screwed.

"I assume that without a vehicle, we have to walk out of here," President Ballinger said to Moretti.

"That's about the size of it, sir," confirmed Moretti. "Daylight's about two and a half hours away. I'm hoping that before then, we'll come within range of a cell tower so that we can call for help. Although I don't know for sure, I assume that there's cellular coverage in this area. Otherwise the mines or maintenance for the wind turbines would have to use a satellite link to communicate with the outside world. Anyway, there's a good chance of there being a tower on the Chinese side of the border—so the closer we get, the better our chances of being able to call for help."

"And if we can't contact anyone before daybreak, we'll be easy prey," said Ballinger, stating the obvious.

Moretti replied, "Yes, sir. It'll be game over."

"I just might have a better alternative," suggested the president. When he explained what he had in mind, Moretti wondered why he hadn't thought of it earlier. They filled in Han Li and President Liu, who both agreed that it was their best chance for survival. Walking in single file with Moretti in the lead, the four of them turned and headed deeper into the Inner Mongolian countryside.

The alarm startled the Chinese army colonel, who immediately dropped his dog-eared *Playboy* magazine and looked at his computer. On the screen was a pulsating red dot, five miles south of the Inner Mongolia border. Displayed next to the red dot was the cell number for which he'd been ordered to search. Since the colonel's unit was responsible for the covert tracking of all wireless phones within China and the border area of surrounding countries, location requests were the norm. However, this directive had come directly from Ren Shi, who had ordered the colonel to ignore his other duties until he found the exact whereabouts of this cell phone.

Typing a series of commands on his keyboard, the colonel brought up the latitude and longitude of the tower that had received the cellular signal, along with its technical specs. He was surprised that the exact location of the device wasn't in the displayed data. Most cell phones contained a GPS chip so that the user could be found in an emergency. Either someone had disabled that capability or this phone didn't have that feature.

Looking at the specs, the colonel saw that this tower was a special use system designed for remote locations such as border crossings. Since these sites didn't handle a large volume of voice or data traffic, they needed access only to the internet and a cellular provider. Thus they had only half the power of standard cellular transmitters, which were much more expensive and unnecessary in remote areas. The specs also indicated that this tower's effective range was ten to eleven miles, which meant that the cell phone for which the colonel was looking had to be within that radius.

The colonel reached across his desk and picked up a small piece of paper, and then nervously dialed the phone number he'd been given less than half a day earlier. When the other party answered, the colonel took a deep breath and explained what he knew.

Ren Shi had just gone to bed when he heard his cell phone ring, and he desperately wanted to ignore it. He'd gotten very little rest in the previous two days, and he didn't want to appear haggard in his televised address to the nation. This would arguably be the most important speech of his life, and he needed his wits about him.

He didn't recognize the phone number displayed on his phone, but that didn't necessarily mean anything. Many senior officials with whom Ren Shi had never spoken before assuming his current duties now called and sought his advice. Since he didn't believe anyone would be foolish enough to contact him at this hour unless it was extremely important, he reluctantly sat up and answered his phone.

Hearing the colonel's voice, Ren Shi expected him to report that he'd been unable to locate Moretti's or Han Li's phone. Based on Wang Lei's description of the crash and subsequent fire, Ren Shi didn't expect that any device would have survived. Instead, the colonel informed him that just minutes earlier, Moretti's phone had connected to a cell tower five miles south of the Inner Mongolian border.

With adrenaline suddenly pumping through his body, Ren Shi threw off the covers and started pacing the room. "You're telling me that the phone is active and that it's in China?"

"It's active, sir, but not in China. That tower has a coverage radius of only ten to eleven miles. If the user was on our side of the border, I would also have detected this signal at a more powerful tower. Because reception is intermittent and weak, the device is at the maximum recognition range for the tower. Therefore I estimate that this cell phone is five to six miles on the Inner Mongolian side of the border. Unfortunately the phone has no GPS capability, so I can't be more precise."

"Have there been any calls to or from that phone number?" Apprehensive, Ren Shi knew he needed to ask this question—but he feared the answer.

"None," replied the colonel. "It's possible that the user might not realize that he has established a cellular connection. He's probably in a fringe area where signal reception fades in and out."

"Find the exact location of the phone. Call me the second you know more," ordered Ren Shi, terminating the call before he received a response. Then he pressed a speed dial number on his cell, turned on the overhead light, and nervously paced the room as he waited.

It took two attempts before Wang Lei answered, half asleep and irritated at being awakened.

Without preamble, Ren Shi asked, "Can you tell me why Moretti's phone just connected with a cell tower?"

Waking up slowly, Wang Lei took several deep breaths before sitting up and calmly responding, "How do you know that?"

"One of our cell towers detected its signal. The connection is intermittent, but this occurred *after* Moretti and his phone should have been crushed and burned to cinders."

"Don't you think he'd summon help if he could use his phone?" suggested Wang Lei. "My guess is that he threw it out the window of his vehicle to make sure we couldn't use it to track him. After all, that pickup didn't drive itself into the pit. Nothing and nobody could have survived that crash and the resulting fire. I'll retrieve the bodies at first light and then work with your tech to find the phone. I've already ordered the mine closed for the day to ensure that Kundek and I can retrieve the bodies in private."

"Good plan, wrong timetable," said Ren Shi. "I want you both to get to that pit right now and personally verify that everyone's favorite boy is in the wreckage. You should have done that earlier."

Wang Lei calmly explained, "The reason I didn't is that I know from experience that the road into the pit is unnavigable at night, even using a vehicle's high beams. There are no safety rails or lighting to keep someone from going over the edge as the road corkscrews its way downward. I consider myself fortunate to have survived my one trip into that mine. But I've lost several vehicles because their drivers thought that since I did it, they could too. Two missed a turn, and a third got too close to the soft shoulder, which gave way under the vehicle's weight. Daylight is less than three hours away. Why not wait until then?"

Ren Shi was far beyond being receptive to excuses. He needed to know whether the four witnesses to what had occurred were still alive—and if they were, he wanted them killed before they could speak to anyone. In a tone of voice that didn't invite further argument, he said, "We can't wait. Dangerous or not, I need you to go into that pit and tell me if they're there. After you've done that, find the phone."

The nine giant Vestas V90 wind turbines stretched for a mile along the top of the hill. The base of each tower weighed 152 tons, soared 262 feet into the air, and was anchored 30 feet into the ground with more than 1,000 tons of concrete and steel rebar. Atop each was an enclosed 75-ton nacelle that housed the gearbox, generator, drive train, and brake assembly. A 40-ton, 148-foot blade assembly increased the height of the structure to nearly 41 stories.

Moretti used the LED lights on top of the 1.8-megawatt machines to guide the four of them to their destination. Getting from the pit to the wind turbines took some time, given the weakened physical state of both presidents and the harshness of the terrain. When they arrived at the southernmost Vestas, Han Li picked the lock on the steel door and they entered.

The interior was bathed in low-level LED lighting, allowing them to find a place in the equipment-laden interior where the presidents could sit and rest. Spotting several cases of bottled water against the right interior wall, Moretti handed out half-liter bottles. Taking one for himself, he sat on the concrete floor beside President Ballinger.

"How are you feeling, sir?" Moretti asked.

"Like an old man, but happy to be alive. President Liu and I would be dead if not for the tremendous tenacity displayed by you and Han Li."

Moretti wasn't good at taking compliments, so he decided to change the subject. "Sir, on the way here you told me that you toured a number of wind turbine farms while you were governor of Kansas and later as the state's senator. If you recall, can you tell me what's above us?" He remembered that the president was known to have a photographic memory.

The president looked around, and then pointed to his right. "That ladder should lead to an elevator that is approximately three stories above us. I'm certain of that because, not being in the best of shape, my legs hurt like hell after climbing the three-story ladder in a similar Vestas tower. The elevator ends three stories from the top at something called the yaw section, which apparently contains a mechanism to keep the turbines facing the wind. The level above that is the nacelle, which contains the power-generating equipment that's connected to the wind turbine blades. On top, and to the rear of the nacelle, is a helicopter pad."

"I'm curious," said Moretti. "How do they get a large piece

of equipment to the top of the tower, since the elevator is three stories above us and ends a similar distance from the yaw section?"

Ballinger explained, "Two rectangular hydraulic hatches extend across the top of the nacelle. Equipment can easily be brought in or removed by helicopter or crane through that opening."

Just as he was about to say something, Moretti shifted his weight and felt the phone dig into his hip. He took it out of his pocket and looked at the screen, but no reception bar was visible. Then it occurred to him that he might be in the perfect place to receive a signal. "I'm going up top," he told the president. "At that height, I might have line of sight with a cell tower. If so, we may yet get out of here alive."

"I'll go with you," Ballinger said. "I'm the only one here who's familiar with the guts of one of these things."

Moretti wanted to say no. Two three-story climbs without a safety harness wasn't a good idea, but he wasn't about to argue with the president of the United States. "After you, sir."

The drive into the inky-dark abyss of the pit was even more harrowing than Wang Lei remembered. Although their SUV had four-wheel drive, the thin tread on their street tires had difficulty adhering to the loose-dirt pathway and maneuvering the tight corkscrew curves along their steep descent. On half a dozen occasions, Wang Lei was certain that Kundek was about to veer off the side of the road and that they'd plunge to their deaths.

Twenty minutes after they started, they reached the floor of the mine. Although the surface could technically be considered flat, it was anything but level. Driving over the large uneven gouges in the earth, dug out by monstrous excavators, was difficult and not unlike traversing the pastureland. It took them longer than anticipated to reach the blackened remains of the pickup.

The crushed vehicle that Wang Lei saw in the headlights was resting upside down. He and Kundek retrieved flashlights from the back of the SUV and walked to the charred steel frame, which was still smoldering from the fire. The industrialist got down on his knees and pointed his light into the front and rear cabs, expecting to see four corpses broken and burned beyond all but forensic recognition. Instead, he saw only charred seats and headrests.

Wang Lei immediately knew that he'd been outsmarted. It had been a serious mistake not to examine the wreckage earlier. Nevertheless, if they thought this deception would result in their escape, they were mistaken. Without a vehicle, they had virtually no chance of making it to the border before sunrise. That meant that at first light, the search aircraft would easily spot them. Soon Moretti, Han Li, and the two presidents would be back in custody for a quick execution.

With some trepidation, Wang Lei climbed back in the SUV. Now he was more worried about what he'd tell his co-conspirator than he was about the treacherous drive up the narrow road to the surface. When he finally emerged from the mine pit, he used his satellite phone to inform a furious Ren Shi that all four escapees were probably still alive and that he needed a search aircraft.

Wang Lei thought that was going to solve his problem, but he quickly learned from Ren Shi that the search couldn't wait until morning. So far, Moretti's phone had made only intermittent contact with a cellular tower, but it could establish a stable connection at any moment. That would be catastrophic.

"Just shut down the tower," Wang Lei told Ren Shi.

"Don't you think I've tried?" replied Ren Shi. "The technicians who manage cellular communication in the border area tell me that none of these antiques can be remotely deactivated. Apparently their electronics are so old that they require someone to go to each tower and physically take it off-line. Meanwhile Moretti could establish a stable connection and place a call at any moment."

Wang Lei asked, "Do we know the location of the phone? Mine has a GPS chip."

"Well, this one doesn't, and since it's communicating with only one tower, we can't triangulate an exact location. All they can tell me is that it's about six miles north of the border."

Wang Lei got out of the vehicle and looked around. He was standing at the northern edge of the mine, which he knew was exactly six miles from the Chinese border, roughly the maximum distance from Moretti's phone to the cell tower. Doing a 360-degree sweep of the area, all he saw was blackness, except for a row of obstruction lights that ran across the top of a ridge. He'd seen those lights so many times that he hadn't given them a second thought—until now. "I have an idea where they're hiding," he said.

"Kill them." And with that, Ren Shi ended the call.

The drive to the Vestas took ten minutes. Then Kundek parked the SUV at the base of the northernmost wind turbine tower. He retrieved a ZH-05 integrated assault rifle, extra ammunition clips, and a ring of bump keys from the rear cargo compartment before proceeding to the entrance door. Shining his flashlight on the lock to identify the manufacturer, he selected a bump key and inserted it. With the butt of his gun, he hit the end of the bump key sharply while at the same time applying torque. The lock's driver pins "jumped" for a fraction of a second, which allowed Kundek to throw open the door.

Acting President Houck couldn't get a straight answer out of Ren Shi. He needed the Chinese leader to provide him with details on what his country was doing to find President Ballinger's body, so that it could be brought back to the United States for the pomp and circumstance of a state funeral. Houck also wanted an update on the search for the killers, but Ren Shi was being vague and elusive. Several times during their conversation, Houck offered to send US investigators to aid in the search, but Ren Shi rejected those offers and told him that everything was under control. Houck knew that this nonsensical response wasn't going to cut it with the American people or Congress. If the Chinese wouldn't voluntarily accept his help, by God, he'd force-feed it to them.

Houck then phoned Director Winegar, of the Office of National Intelligence, and asked him to press the seventeen agencies under his control to get him information. Winegar told Houck that they were already analyzing a raft of satellite data, as well as what he termed the "death video." Winegar reported that after a microscopic review and deconstruction analysis by a team of CIA technicians and scientists, the consensus was that President Ballinger had been held hostage in Inner Mongolia.

The CIA had based its conclusion on a brief shot of the grass on which the two presidents were kneeling before the cameraman narrowed the focus to head shots. Using computerized pixel enhancement, botanists had determined that the men were kneeling in feather grass, or *Stipa baicalensis*, which grows only in or around the Chinese cities of Gansu, Hebei, and Jilin, and within the first twenty-five miles on the Inner Mongolian side of its border with China. One of these areas was only a two- to three-hour drive from Beijing, which made it the logical choice as the location in the video.

Houck ordered Winegar to adjust the orbit of whatever satellites were necessary to photograph the Chinese border area with Inner Mongolia. Houck had refused to be sworn in as president until he saw either a video of the actual killing or the recovery of President Ballinger's body. Although he had assumed, along with the rest of the world, that the presidents were dead, he needed something more than an assumption before taking office. Nevertheless, he was also painfully aware of the constitutional crisis that he was causing, so he needed clarification quickly.

Moretti followed President Ballinger up the thirty-foot ladder that led from the topmost elevator platform to the equipment room just below the nacelle. Both men were dripping in sweat, and each had their issues. The president's legs felt like Jell-O from the nearly six stories he'd climbed so far, and Moretti's back was in full spasm, making it painful for him to raise a leg from one rung of the ladder to the next.

When they reached the yaw section, the president threw open the grate above him, hit the light switch beside it, and entered. Right behind him, Moretti pulled his cell phone from his pocket as he stepped onto the steel planking. He had hoped to be able to get a steady signal from this elevated platform, but one look at his screen told him otherwise.

"Any luck?" the president asked.

"The signal's intermittent at best, sir, and it doesn't stay active even long enough for me to dial a number."

"You might have a better chance if you go up to the nacelle and open the large overhead service hatches. If there's a cell tower in the vicinity, you should connect with it. You can open the hatches by throwing the activation switch below the hatch on the right. I'm going to stay here. I'm exhausted, and these legs can't climb another step."

Moretti helped the president lower himself to the floor and lean back against the wall. Once he was as comfortable as he could be, sitting on metal planking with his back against a steel tube, Moretti slowly climbed the ladder. The stabbing pain in his back continued, causing him to grit his teeth.

In contrast to the yaw section, which was relatively empty, the nacelle was crammed with equipment. The faint glow of light from various LED control panels and displays allowed Moretti to see the bulky outlines of the gearbox and generator, which were directly in front of him and in tandem with each other. Moretti wiped the perspiration off his face with the sleeve of his jacket, and then pulled the phone from his pocket. He fully expected to be able to establish a solid connection from this height. There had to be a tower in the area; otherwise he wouldn't have received any signal at all. As logical as that argument seemed, however, his phone still didn't register a single bar.

Moretti walked over to the switch that the president had mentioned and pressed it, hoping that opening the hatches would make a difference. As the area above his head gradually transformed into a pincushion of lights, he raised his arm and saw that he *did* have a signal, which lasted slightly longer than at the base of the tower. However, it was still intermittent and not steady enough to establish a connection. Frustrated, he turned to close the hatches. As he did so, he glanced outside and noticed the headlights of an approaching vehicle.

Ren Shi's follow-up call with Acting President Houck did not go well. He sought to placate his American counterpart with an even longer list of fictitious actions he'd taken to locate the president's body and find those responsible for his murder, but his efforts fell on deaf ears, much as they had an hour earlier. Ren Shi's goal was to ensure that the Americans would eventually accept that their president's body would never be found. China would receive criticism for this, but he would point out that his country had lost its president and four ministers, whose bodies also had not been recovered.

Houck had called the second time to inform Ren Shi that a US intelligence agency had determined that the presidents had been held within a twenty-five-mile-wide band of land in the Inner Mongolia border region, which was where the search for their bodies should be focused.

Ren Shi wondered, *How in the hell did they figure that out?* He had no doubt that a US reconnaissance satellite would eventually put the entire area under a microscope—which meant that he had to immediately resolve the situation with Moretti, Han Li, and the presidents. He didn't believe this surveillance was yet in place, because he knew from experience that it took hours to coordinate and move a satellite's orbit. Also, Ren Shi's minister of defense had informed him that none of the American spy satellites were currently over Inner Mongolia.

Wang Lei needed to get his act together and quickly kill four people who should already be dead. If the presidents were photographed by one of those high-resolution satellite marvels, there'd be no holding the Americans back from using whatever force was necessary to rescue them. If that happened, the Communist Party would make sure that Ren Shi didn't live out the day.

Ren Shi dispatched a military helicopter to assist Wang Lei, making it clear to the pilot that the search window was very short. The pilot, with whom he'd worked before, was told that he'd be paid a fortune for this off-the-books mission if he did three things. First, search the designated area for four people. Second, keep his mouth shut about what he did or saw; this mission never existed. And third, if called upon to expend his ordnance, do so without hesitation. Meanwhile, Ren Shi had already taken action to ensure that the pilot and his aircraft would never make it back to Beijing, regardless of the outcome of this search.

Given the choice, he wanted visual confirmation of four dead bodies *before* the American satellite was in place. However, failing that, he'd employ his insurance policy. Four military aircraft filled with incendiary devices were prepared to firebomb the region extending from the silver mine to five miles south of the Chinese border. This would ensure not only that those he was searching for were dead, but also that Wang Lei, Kundek, and anyone else involved would also be killed.

If questioned, Ren Shi would say that the firebombing was done to kill those who had beheaded the presidents, and to do so before they had time to scatter and escape. He would claim that he had relied on solid intelligence in making that decision. No one would have an issue with that order. Both nations wanted those who'd killed their president dead by whatever means necessary, and he was more than happy to take credit on the world stage for making that happen.

CHAPTER

15

M ajor Doug Cray rubbed his weary eyes and leaned back in his chair, careful not to bump his head on the wall close behind him. His office at INSCOM, the US Army Intelligence and Security Command, at Fort Belvoir, Virginia, could more appropriately be described as a cubicle with high walls and a ceiling. Although he was a major, that rank was not exceptional on a base that had twice as many employees as the Pentagon and was home to sixteen military organizations.

On the right-hand side of his desk was a neat stack of papers that would take well into the evening to clear, but Cray hadn't touched a single page for the past hour. All he could think about was his friend Matt Moretti. He'd learned from a Secret Service report that Moretti and Han Li were last seen leaving their hotel after assaulting a People's Liberation Army officer and his men who'd gone there to arrest them. That was nearly twenty-four hours ago. The major didn't know why the Chinese Army was after them; in fact, not even the State Department could get a clear answer on that. But he figured there was one person who knew, so he decided to call and see if Moretti needed any help.

When Cray dialed Moretti's cell phone, there was a lengthy pause followed by a *failed call* indication on his screen. When he fared no better on his second and third attempts, he decided to turn to the geek side of his command—the cyber-espionage unit—and task them with locating Moretti's cell phone. This wasn't the first time he'd asked for help from the mostly twenty-year-olds, who occupied a room filled with high-tech equipment in the basement of the building. On more than a few occasions, despite starting with only a thread of information, they had ferreted out what he needed and ultimately been responsible for preventing foreign and homegrown terrorist attacks. Today that thread was a cell phone number half a world away that had no discernible receptivity.

Just two hours after making his request, the major received a call from one of the geeks. She informed him that the phone in question was currently in intermittent contact with a low-power Chinese cell tower exactly 5.1267 miles south of the China–Inner Mongolian border. However, the signal wasn't strong enough for the user to either place or receive calls. She then provided the longitude and latitude of the tower, which he wrote down.

Cray's mind darted back to a CIA report he'd read only two hours earlier, which said that the abducted presidents of the United States and China had most likely been held hostage in that same region. He brought up an archived military satellite photo of the border area, found the referenced tower, and superimposed a circle around it at the distance he'd been given. The circumference seemed to run through a large mining pit, pastureland, and a wind turbine farm. Knowing Moretti's and Han Li's penchant for uncovering the truth long before anyone else, he wondered what they were up to.

It was seven in the evening when Major General Thomas Scharlau, commander of INSCOM, gathered his papers off the conference room table. He had started his day thirteen hours earlier and was looking forward to going home and pouring himself a tall Tito's and tonic. But first he had to go to the latrine to empty his bladder of six cups of coffee, which is what it had taken him to stay awake during the budget and finance marathon that had just ended.

Just as he started in the direction of the latrine, Scharlau's cell phone rang. Looking at the screen, he saw that the caller's ID was blocked, which was standard for all cell phones used in his command. Prioritizing his needs, he let the call go to voice mail. If it was important, the caller would leave a message or send him a text. When he returned to his office a few minutes later to retrieve his belongings and lock up, he suspected that the caller was the major now standing in front of his office door.

"I think I've located Moretti," Cray said.

The major general took a seat in one of the two chairs in front of his desk, turned it to face the other, and told Cray to sit down. "I'm sure you know that the Chinese government wants to arrest both Moretti and Han Li for interfering with their investigation, as well as decking a People's Liberation Army officer and his men," Scharlau said. "I hope he has a colorful explanation for these extracurricular activities because the secretary of defense wants his head on a pike— and since he works for me, mine alongside it. Where exactly is he?"

"His cell signal is too weak for us to communicate with him. But as best we can tell, he's in Inner Mongolia, a little over five miles north of the Chinese border."

"Where the presidents were thought to be held," Scharlau said. "How in the hell did he figure that out?"

"Sir?"

"Moretti and Han Li have been no less than amazing in coming up with every important investigative find on these abductions. I'm not sure how they do it, but I'm willing to bet they have a good idea of the location of the presidents' bodies—and possibly the whereabouts of the kidnappers too. As of now, all command resources are at your disposal, and your only responsibility is getting in touch with Moretti. While you're at it, make sure that Jack Bonaquist is aware of what you're doing. He's as good an agent as there is in the Secret Service, and I owe him more than a few favors. Unless I'm mistaken, his ass is on the fast track to retirement, and he could use all the help he can get."

"Understood, sir," Cray said. He stood, came to attention, and left.

Moretti left the nacelle and returned to the yaw section, where he found the president still sitting with his back against the steel wall.

"Any luck?" President Ballinger asked.

"I still can't connect. And when the hatches were open, I saw an approaching vehicle—as if we didn't already have enough problems. We need to get President Liu and Han Li up here, in case whoever that is decides to search this tower. If we're lucky, they won't bother inspecting the upper sections."

"Do you really expect them to be that negligent?"

"They're time constrained," replied Moretti. "With daylight fast approaching, they'll want to start searching the pastureland between the mine and the border, figuring that we're trying to get back to China. I don't believe they'd expect us to back ourselves into a corner by taking refuge in a wind turbine from which there's only one exit. They're probably searching the towers only because it's night and they want to check them off their list of possible hiding places."

"Makes sense," agreed Ballinger.

"In a few minutes, we'll find out if theory and practice match," said Moretti. Then he cupped his hands and yelled down to Han Li, informing her of the approaching vehicle. Waiting by the elevator, he saw the light in the equipment area at the base of the tower go out and heard them climbing the ladder to the lower platform.

A short time later, a clearly exhausted President Liu walked off the elevator followed by Han Li. Moretti stepped inside and pulled the emergency button on the control panel, thereby locking the elevator in place. He hoped that anyone searching the tower would believe it was out of order and would not want to climb twenty-six stories to investigate the upper levels.

When they entered the yaw section, Moretti pulled his cell

from his pocket and saw that the screen was dark. He pressed the power switch several times, but nothing changed. His cell had died and was of no more use than Han Li's, which had earlier expended the last of its power. Now that they didn't have a working phone, there was no way anyone would know where they were. Any chance of being rescued was gone. They were as good as dead.

Kundek bumped the lock on the final wind tower and threw open the steel door. With his assault rifle slung over his shoulder, and holding a flashlight in one hand and his handgun in the other, the giant Mongolian cautiously entered. He'd probed the other Vestas from base to nacelle, and he expected this search to be as fruitless as the previous eight. But his pessimism quickly evaporated when he noticed the two empty water bottles on the floor, something he hadn't seen in the other towers. They could have been left behind by a maintenance crew too lazy to police after themselves, but the drops of water on the floor beside them suggested otherwise.

After turning on the interior base lighting and finding no one hiding behind the equipment racks, Kundek grabbed a rung on the ladder leading to the first platform and began to climb. When he arrived, he was surprised to see that the elevator wasn't there. Since the only other place it stopped was twenty-six stories above him, that meant that either it was broken or someone had disabled it. Given the presence of the empty water bottles and his own lack of faith in coincidence, there was no question in the Mongolian's mind that he'd found the presidents.

Placing his handgun in the small of his back, Kundek went to the interior tower wall and began to climb the series of rungs that extended from the base to the yaw section. Without a safety line there was no margin for error as he made his ascent, so he gripped each rung a little tighter than he normally would have. Kundek considered himself in excellent shape, but just short of the halfway point his right leg began to cramp so badly that he thought he might slip and fall. He was sweating profusely and rapidly becoming dehydrated, which further increased his muscular fatigue. He wished he'd taken the time to gulp down a bottle of water before he started, but hindsight was always 20/20.

As he climbed, Kundek thought about the prosperity that he'd been promised. Women, drink, and leisure activities would punctuate each day. All he had to do was kill the four people who were hiding somewhere above him, and then that life would be his.

The Harbin Z-9B appeared on the horizon just as dawn was breaking. Wang Lei immediately recognized the military utility helicopter, a variant of the French Dauphin Eurocopter. His company manufactured the air-to-ground missiles that it carried, as well as the two fixed 23-mm Type 23-2 cannons that protruded from it. As he watched the forty-foot-long, thirteen-foot-high helicopter approach, his satellite phone rang. It was the aircraft commander asking where he should begin his search pattern.

Instead of providing instructions, Wang Lei directed him to set down fifty yards from the southernmost wind turbine tower. When the helicopter landed, a short man who probably weighed 150 pounds soaking wet exited the aircraft and gave Wang Lei a crisp salute. He reported that his orders were to search the surrounding area for four people and upon detection to report their position to Wang Lei. He also said that he was told not to ask any questions and to follow orders without hesitation. Wang confirmed those instructions, adding that the only change in the plan was that Wang was going too.

After helping to strap Wang Lei in, the pilot took his seat at the controls and lifted the helicopter smoothly off the ground. It rose to a height of two hundred feet and at Wang Lei's direction began its grid pattern at the eastern edge of the coal mine. The industrialist didn't give Kundek a second thought, believing that the presidents were no more likely to be in the ninth wind turbine than in the first eight. In hindsight, that assumption proved to be the falling domino that changed the course of history.

After six hours of nonstop digging, Afridi began to doubt that he'd ever get out of this tomb. His fingers were raw and bleeding from removing pile after pile of rubble from one of the side exits. His followers were doing the same at the other portals, but so far there was not a ray of sunlight or a whiff of air to show for their efforts. It seemed as if the entire mountain had cascaded down upon them. If that was true, this was where their corporal bodies would spend eternity.

Afridi looked down at the strips of cloth wrapped around his bleeding hands. They were flayed and tattered, soaked in blood from the jagged rocks and debris. After wiping the sweat from his brow, he tore two more pieces of cloth from his rapidly disintegrating shirt, replaced the wraps on his hands, and continued digging. For the next two hours, despite his increasing despair, he pulled aside one rock after the other without looking up. If he failed to escape, it wouldn't be because of a lack of trying.

He was so focused on his efforts that he didn't hear the cries of joy from those around him. It took several attempts by one of his followers, pulling on Afridi's shoulders, to finally force him to stop digging. Then he saw that everyone was pointing toward a faint glow of daylight. Reenergized by that pinpoint of hope, he took the lead in widening the hole until it was large enough for him to crawl out of the cave. Embraced by the warmth of the sun, Afridi stood, took in a deep breath of the cold mountain air, and scanned the landscape before him. Despite opening and closing his eyes several times, he failed to reset the image before him. Afridi had absolutely no idea where he was.

When he heard the helicopter approach and set down, Moretti guessed that Wang Lei had asked for help and gotten it in spades. As troubling as this was, his immediate problem was that someone had thrown back the entry grate into the yaw section. Fortunately he'd gotten everyone into the nacelle, where the clutter of equipment gave them an opportunity to hide and defend themselves.

Moretti positioned the presidents on the floor behind the heavy steel plate of the gearbox, and he and Han Li stood with their Norinco Type 92 handguns aimed at the only entrance into the nacelle. If they were lucky, they'd kill whoever poked their head above the grate. At least, that was the plan.

What actually occurred was far different. The hatch flew up with such speed and force that it momentarily startled them, and in that split second an assault rifle rose through the opening. As soon as they saw it, Moretti and Han Li both dove down to the steel floor and scurried for cover. The burst of gunfire that followed spewed a stream of bullets throughout the enclosure, giving Kundek time to step onto the deck unchallenged.

Moretti looked up and saw the giant Mongolian pointing an assault rifle at him. Even more distressing, when he hit the metal floor, his own handgun had come loose and slid two feet away. If he went for it, he'd have half a dozen bullets in him before he could touch it. Defenseless, Moretti had no doubt that he was going to die. He wondered if he'd feel any pain, or if his thought processes would just suddenly cease.

As Moretti pondered his own death, Han Li's foot connected with the left side of Kundek's head. An instant later, her other foot came around and smashed into his right temple, causing him to momentarily lose his balance and stagger backward. Moretti was certain that either kick would have cracked open anyone else's skull—or at least rendered him unconscious. But the Mongolian just shook his head and then sent a three-bullet barrage at the spot Han Li had occupied just a split second earlier, missing her by less than an inch. Han Li was forced to use the surrounding equipment for cover as she retreated toward the front of the nacelle.

As this was unfolding, Moretti grabbed his gun. With no

time to precisely aim, he sent a round in Kundek's direction, trying to pull the Mongolian's focus away from Han Li and back to himself. The good and bad news was that it worked. Kundek took his eyes off Han Li, but then he quickly put two bullets into the ex–Army Ranger's left shoulder, sending him sprawling on his back. But Kundek couldn't get off a kill shot because at that moment, a string of bullets hit the floor and wall around the giant, forcing him to dive for cover.

Moretti assumed that Han Li had been his savior, but when he turned and looked behind him, he saw President Ballinger holding a rifle. The president started toward Moretti, but then he saw Kundek picking himself up off the deck. In a rush to get back to his hiding place, Ballinger dropped the gun that Han Li had earlier given him. Then he tripped over it, accidentally kicking it out of reach underneath an adjacent equipment cabinet.

With the president unarmed, the Mongolian kicked Moretti's gun far out of reach. Content that Moretti was defenseless and wounded, Kundek then decided to come back and finish him off after he killed the presidents. But just as Kundek stepped over Moretti, heading for Han Li, the ex–Army Ranger balled his right hand into a fist and drove it into the Mongolian's balls. Kundek made a guttural sound, and the look on his face was an inhuman combination of pain and hatred.

Switching his rifle to his left hand, Kundek bent over and removed a seven-inch knife from a scabbard strapped to his calf. Moretti tried to get away, but before he could, Kundek plunged the blade deep into his back. The pain wasn't as bad as Moretti expected, considering that a piece of steel was wedged so far into his body that he was surprised it didn't come out the other side. But the shock to his system made him feel increasingly light-headed and detached from his physical surroundings. *So this is what it's like to die,* he thought. As his vision began to narrow and fade, and he began to lose consciousness, Moretti saw an angel rise behind Kundek and spread her wings. A moment later, he felt nothing.

Kundek released his grip on the knife and looked at the gearbox behind which he had seen President Ballinger take cover. His balls hurt so badly, and he was so intent on killing the presidents, that he didn't notice Han Li until it was too late. In a lightning-fast move, she brought her knee back to her chest and violently slammed her foot into the left side of his torso several times in rapid succession, stopping only when she heard his ribs cracking. She followed this assault with a snap kick into each kneecap, crushing both patellas. Screaming in pain and gasping for air, Kundek reached out and grabbed her shirt as he collapsed to the decking.

Once on the steel planking, he rolled his massive weight on top of Han Li. Pinned and unable to move, all she could do was watch as he clenched his bear-sized right hand and hit her in the solar plexus, knocking the air out of her. He then grabbed her throat with both hands and squeezed with every ounce of strength he had left. He could see that she was close to unconsciousness, when suddenly something hit him on the side of his head.

Han Li heard a gunshot and felt the vise around her neck release. Looking at Kundek's face, she saw a gaping hole just under his right ear. Pushing his bloody head aside and working her way out from under his body, she saw Moretti a few feet away. He was lying on his right side with Kundek's rifle in his hand and the knife still protruding from his back. With blood dripping from his lips, he tried to tell her something. Han Li ran to him, but before Moretti could utter a word, the expression on his face froze. Then she heard the helicopter return.

CHAPTER

16

Placing her hand below Moretti's nose, Han Li was surprised to find that he was still breathing. She wished there was something she could do, but with a knife in his back and two bullets in his shoulder, only a surgeon—and a great deal of luck—could save his life. Considering they were at the top of a wind turbine in the middle of an Inner Mongolian pasture, lacking any means of transportation or communication, and being hunted by a maniacal industrialist, she thought Moretti's chances of surviving were almost nonexistent.

Moretti's odds of survival moved even closer to zero when Han Li considered that her first responsibility was the safety of the two presidents. If they had an opportunity to escape the tower, she'd have to leave Moretti behind. He would slow them down significantly. She had feelings for him, more than she cared to admit, although she had never told him so. But she also understood that if their situations were reversed, he would prioritize the presidents' safety above trying to save her life.

As she moved to retrieve her handgun and rifle, Han Li noticed the green hatch release light glowing in the semi-darkness. As she approached the presidents, who sat with their backs against the gearbox, she said, "President Ballinger, you said that you are somewhat familiar with wind turbines."

"I know a little about them from the VIP tours I've taken," the president said, "but nothing technical."

"Am I correct in assuming that there's no way out of here other than through the door at the base of the wind turbine?" asked Han Li.

"There's also the helicopter pad on top of the nacelle, but that's it," said Ballinger.

"I suspect that no one knows we're hiding in this tower, and that the helicopter is searching the pastureland for us because they still think we're headed for the Chinese border. It's also reasonable to assume that it's a well-armed military aircraft, since the people hunting us don't seem to want us alive. If we destroy or damage that helicopter, we might be able to take the Mongolian's SUV and make it to the border."

"How do you plan to destroy the helicopter?" President Liu asked.

She pointed to the assault rifle lying next to Moretti and said, "By using that to take out its tail rotor."

"Do you think it has the range or power?" President Ballinger asked, looking at the weapon. "Why not try to kill the pilot instead?"

"I'll have to focus on either the pilot or the rotor because I won't have time for both. There's no way to know, before I take that shot, if the cockpit is bulletproof or the pilot is wearing a projectile-resistant vest. The rotor's an open target."

"But how will you draw it in close enough to take the shot?" President Ballinger asked. "They're not going to approach if they see a weapon in your hand."

"We open these hatches so the helicopter pilot can clearly see me," said President Liu, in a firm voice that indicated he'd made up his mind.

"I think it'd be more enticing if he saw both of us," President Ballinger suggested.

"Even better," said President Liu. "If the pilot hasn't been told that we're still alive, he'll be confused and want to take a closer look. Even if he's part of this, my guess is that he'll still hesitate before pulling the trigger, which will give Han Li more time."

"We hope," added Ballinger.

Han Li didn't like the idea of the presidents risking their lives, but she understood that ultimately it made no difference. If she was unable to disable the rotor, they were all dead anyway. She retrieved the assault rifle and found a spare clip of ammunition on Kundek's body. Positioning herself to the rear of the hatch opening, she announced that she was ready. A moment later President Ballinger pressed the green button and both nacelle hatches slowly began to open.

The Harbin Z-9B helicopter was on the next leg of its search pattern, and heading straight for the southernmost wind turbine, when the nacelle doors opened and revealed two men dressed in orange jumpsuits. The pilot hovered the aircraft fifty yards from the tower, where—judging by the look on his face—he apparently recognized the two unkempt men who were staring at him. It would be impossible not to recognize them, since their photos in orange jumpsuits were on every form of media throughout the country.

Wang Lei was astounded that the presidents were still alive. Kundek had entered this tower less than half an hour earlier, which probably meant that he was dead. At this stage of the operation, Wang Lei considered Kundek's death good news, since he'd planned to get rid of him within the week anyway. The Mongolian had been privy to too many of Wang Lei's secrets.

"Those are the men I've been searching for," Wang Lei said to the pilot. "Fire a missile into that tower and bring it down."

"I'm not going to kill the president of China," said the pilot, just before Wang Lei put a bullet into his head and took control of the helicopter.

An adept pilot, the industrialist concentrated on the task at hand. He flipped the aircraft's weapons safety switch off, dipped the nose, set his laser sighting at the base of the tower, and pressed the launch button. The Z-9B bucked as an FGM-148 Javelin air-to-ground missile streaked from the aircraft. An instant later, a thunderous explosion was heard and a curtain of fire, dust, and debris rose in front of him.

The explosion rocked the tower, and the presidents were thrown backward onto the floor. The missile resulted in a four-foot hole of bent and broken rebar, impregnated with chunks of concrete, half a dozen feet from the base of the tower. But the gargantuan structure, anchored by a thousand tons of steel, barely noticed the attack.

Han Li believed that the pilot, upon seeing the small amount of damage he'd inflicted, would decide not to take the tower down, and instead concentrate his attack on the open nacelle. As it turned out, that assumption was correct. She watched as the helicopter adjusted its position and dipped its nose so that its missiles pointed directly into the elongated structure at the top of the tower.

Just as Wang Lei brought the helicopter into firing position, Han Li came out of hiding. In one smooth motion, she flipped the rifle's assault selector switch to full auto, rested the gun on the open edge of the nacelle hatch, and pressed the trigger. In no more time than it took to snap one's finger, every round from the magazine left the gun barrel and hit the aircraft. Unfortunately they all ricocheted off the tail section and the rotor remained undamaged.

Wang Lei jerked the helicopter up and relocated his hover point a mile further away from the nacelle. At that distance, Han Li knew she had no chance of damaging the aircraft. She also realized that for a missile, a mile was an insignificant distance. Its impact would obliterate the nacelle and instantly kill everyone inside. She didn't bother to take cover, since there was nothing she could do to prevent her death. Soon she was joined by the presidents, as they all three stood and defiantly faced their executioner.

As she waited, Han Li was startled by an impossibly fast streak of white light that hit the attack helicopter. In the blink of an eye, the aircraft exploded in a fireball and plummeted to earth. At the same time, Chinese fighters roared overhead, releasing four missiles that apparently hit airborne targets on the horizon. The resulting explosions threw red-and-orange fireballs high into the sky.

Once the airspace was clear, two Z-10s, China's premier attack helicopter, and two Z-8 transports, each capable of carrying up to twenty-seven troops, approached. Three of the aircraft set down not far from the tower, while a Z-8 landed on the helicopter pad behind the nacelle. Its skids had barely touched the deck when the side door flew open and Bonaquist stepped out, followed by Lieutenant Colonel Yan He.

"Mr. President, are you and President Liu all right, sir?" asked Bonaquist as he approached President Ballinger.

"We're fine, Jack."

"Then we need to get you both into the helicopter, so that we can get you to safety."

Behind her, Han Li could hear Yan He also directing President Liu to get on board.

"We need to get Moretti to a hospital immediately. Otherwise he'll die," Ballinger said in an authoritative tone, pointing to a motionless body. Bonaquist had been too busy trying to coax the president into the waiting helicopter to notice the ex–Army Ranger lying facedown with a knife protruding from his back.

Kneeling beside Moretti, Bonaquist felt his carotid artery and detected a faint pulse. "We'll have one of the other helicopters transport him, sir."

"Like hell we will, every second counts. Moretti's life is hanging by a thread. Put him in my copter—now! That's an order."

While Ballinger was laying down the law to Bonaquist, President Liu was having a similar conversation with Yan He, which he summarily ended with an imperious wave of his hand. Then Liu walked over to Ballinger and said, "I heard what you said, and I agree. You and I will both go with him to make sure he gets the priority medical attention he deserves."

"Thank you," replied Ballinger. Following the conversation with their respective presidents, Bonaquist and Yan He went up to the landing pad and retrieved a stretcher from the helicopter. They then gently lifted Moretti off the floor, placed him facedown on the stretcher, with the knife still protruding from his back, and carried him to the waiting Z-8. Once on board, they lowered the stretcher onto the steel decking and covered him with two thick blankets.

When everyone was strapped into their seats, Yan He directed the aircraft commander to lift off. Protected by two Z-10s and the Chinese fighters circling overhead, they headed back to Beijing. As the aircraft gained altitude, the lieutenant colonel went into the cockpit and told the pilot to put the pedal to the metal. Then he directed the copilot, a young captain, to get the location of the nearest hospital. Quickly checking with command headquarters, the copilot gave the aircraft commander a heading to the closest hospital and then connected Yan He to a military trauma surgeon.

While Yan He was speaking with the doctor, Bonaquist opened the emergency medical supply locker, which was standard on board all Z-8 troop transport aircraft, and laid out a few supplies. He wasn't an EMT by any stretch of the imagination, but his Secret Service experience had included a fair amount of life support training. As he was doing this, Yan He returned to the rear of the aircraft, plugged a headset into a radio jack in the bulkhead, and handed it to Bonaquist.

Bonaquist warned the trauma surgeon that he was in way over his head and that if he screwed up, he could easily kill Moretti. Brushing that statement aside, the surgeon directed the Secret Service agent to quickly insert two IV lines and an intubation tube into Moretti. As the surgeon explained, there was a greater than 95 percent chance that Moretti would die anyway, so there was little to lose and everything to gain.

Throughout the flight, Moretti's pulse could barely be detected, and everyone knew that he was on the knife's edge of death. When the helicopter landed at the hospital, a team of doctors and nurses rushed into the aircraft. Thirty minutes later they carried Moretti out on a stretcher and placed him on a gurney, with a nurse on either side of him holding IV bags.

As Moretti was wheeled toward the emergency room, he was followed closely by two scruffy-looking men in orange jumpsuits. Everyone's mouths fell open when they realized that those scruffy-looking men were actually President Liu of China and President Ballinger of the United States. Cell phones were quickly pulled from pockets and the two men were heavily photographed following Moretti to the emergency room. Posted online, the photos immediately went viral.

The medical staff frantically worked on Moretti. The good news was that the CT scan showed that the two bullets that had entered his left shoulder had missed the brachial artery, the main blood vessel in the arm. The bad news was that the knife blade had nicked his right lung, causing blood to accumulate in the lung and chest cavity. Because of the prolonged time that it had taken to get him to a hospital, not one medical professional in the room was optimistic that Moretti would survive the surgery ahead of him.

During the operation, both presidents elected to stay in the adjacent waiting room rather than move to a secure location in Beijing. They had endured an enormous amount of anguish during their captivity, and they were mentally and physically exhausted. Even so, no amount of coercion from Yan He and Bonaquist could persuade them to leave. Ballinger and Liu both wanted to be there for Moretti, just as he'd been there for them.

With the presidents' refusal to leave, the Chinese military and the US Secret Service arrived at the hospital in force. They established airtight security in and around the premises, while half a dozen combat helicopters patrolled the skies overhead.

Eight hours after Moretti had arrived at the hospital, the doctor leading the surgical team walked into the waiting room. All eyes were on the tall, lanky surgeon, one of three who had worked on Moretti. Although the look on his weary face was noncommittal, it suggested that the news was not good. Yan He approached him for a brief discussion, and then the surgeon left the room.

"What did he say?" Liu and Ballinger asked in near unison.

"Moretti somehow survived the operation, but he's so weak that he probably won't live much longer. The surgeon asked if he should release the body to US security after Moretti dies. I told him, with your permission," said Yan He, looking at President Liu, "to transfer Moretti's remains to the US ambassador after the death certificate is issued, and to call me if he encounters any problems. I think we've all done as much as we can here."

Both heads of state reluctantly agreed that it was time to leave. Ten minutes later, they were on separate helicopters. President Ballinger was headed to the Beijing International Airport, and President Liu was on his way to the Chinese presidential palace.

Word of the rescue of the two presidents had spread like wildfire. Ren Shi first heard about it in a phone call from General Chien An. Chief of the General Staff of the People's Liberation Army, Chien An was the highest-ranking military officer in the country. He told Ren Shi that he'd authorized the rescue operation without first consulting with him simply because time was of the essence. Ren Shi didn't know if that was true, but it didn't matter. Since the rescue had been an unmitigated success, he didn't dare to utter even the slightest criticism of Chien An, who was now a national hero. Ren Shi's bruised ego took some consolation in the fact that Chien An said that he'd be over shortly to brief him on what had occurred, an unexpected courtesy from the rough-edged general.

As he tried to piece together a path of deniability, Ren Shi wondered if President Liu had any suspicion of his involvement in the abductions. Apparently, based on what the general told him, Wang Lei, Kundek, and any other accomplices associated with the kidnappings were dead. As far as anyone still alive knew, Ren Shi had acted honorably and decisively, especially in retaliating against the extremists who planned the abductions. Wang Lei's use of a military helicopter was a problem, but Ren Shi could probably figure a way to explain that.

Maybe things hadn't worked out so badly after all, thought Ren Shi. A few days ago, he was being pushed out the door. Today, he was all but certain that the Party would name him the new senior vice premier. With his mood improving by the minute, he showered and shaved, and then put on a white shirt, red tie, and dark suit. He'd greet President Liu when the helicopter landed, with the cameras rolling, looking every bit his eventual successor.

General Chien An was sixty four years old. Standing five feet seven, he had a stocky build, thick arms and legs, a neck girth that some compared to a tree trunk, and closely cropped hair that was perpetually black, thanks to the intervention of his barber.

Born and raised on a farm in northeast China, Chien An had learned to read and write from his mother, a schoolteacher in the community. By the age of fifteen, he'd had enough of farming and, lying about his age, joined the army. He had never married, but those who knew him understood that, metaphorically speaking, he considered the army his wife.

A month earlier, Chien An had succeeded General Lin Bogang, who'd committed suicide after receiving a diagnosis of an incurable debilitating illness. At least that was what the government said in their press release. Unofficially, his debilitating illness was a 9-mm round to the back of the head after a failed attempt to overthrow the government.

Before authorizing the rescue operation for the two presidents,

Chien An had received a disturbing call from his former aide, Lieutenant Colonel Yan He. The colonel had informed him that the head of President Ballinger's Secret Service detail had shared with him the details of a CIA report. It seems that an American satellite had determined that the presidents were being held hostage somewhere within a twenty-five-mile-wide strip of land just on the Inner Mongolian side of their border. American intelligence had also picked up an intermittent cellular signal from one of their agents, which led them to believe that the presidents were still alive and approximately five miles on the Inner Mongolian side of the border.

Chien An had bluntly asked Yan He, "Do you believe them?"

"I trust the Secret Service agent," the lieutenant colonel had replied, "and we never actually saw the presidents beheaded."

Chien An wasn't given to rash action, but neither did he typically succumb to paralysis by analysis. Based on what he'd been told, if there was even a slim chance that the presidents were alive, he needed to dispatch a rescue force of combat and transport aircraft to the area. He had thought about informing Ren Shi of his decision, but decided against it since he didn't want to lose the element of surprise. The general didn't trust any politician to keep a secret. He'd take some heat for his unilateral decision to act, but ultimately there was little that anyone in the government could do to him except express their displeasure.

Putting Yan He on hold, Chien An had speed-dialed the commander of the army's Quick Response Force and placed the three of them in conference. As Yan He and the colonel in charge of the QRF worked out the details, Chien An pushed aside the cup of tea in front of him, removed a bottle of Johnny Walker Green and a glass from the cabinet behind his desk, and poured himself a drink. Thirty minutes later, he approved the action plan and ended the conference call.

By the time Lieutenant Colonel Yan He had phoned General Chien An to notify him that both presidents had been rescued, the bottle of scotch was half empty—or half full, depending on one's perspective.

During his flight back to Beijing, President Liu had contacted Chien An on an encrypted military channel and told him what needed to be done. The general listened without comment and acknowledged his orders. He then made three calls in rapid succession, thrown a few mints into his mouth, and left the office.

Air Force One departed the Beijing International Airport to the sound of cheers and clapping within the aircraft. The stewards had given everyone, except the crew and security staff, a glass of champagne just after they were seated. They had two things to celebrate—the president's survival, and the fact that they were returning home. Now they were busy refilling those same glasses as the plane continued its ascent.

Thinking about Moretti, President Ballinger set his celebratory champagne aside. According to the call he had received just before takeoff, the ex–Army Ranger was still holding on, but not expected to survive much longer.

Then, after throwing his orange jumpsuit into the trash bin, the leader of the free world showered and shaved, and put on a tailored dark blue business suit, white shirt, and light blue tie. The speech his staff had prepared was short and to the point, and he made no edits. After a brief read-through, Ballinger looked directly at the camera and delivered his speech. He thanked the American people for their prayers, and he praised the Chinese military and the Secret Service for their successful joint rescue operation. No second take was necessary. Moments later, the video was released to the world press. When the communications crew left his office, the president asked the steward to remove the champagne and replace it with a glass of water.

For the next hour, as President Ballinger sat alone in his Air Force One office and thought about what had happened over the previous four days, he came to see it as a wakeup call. Although the Protectors of Islam hadn't been behind the abductions, any number of radical groups and rogue nation-states were attacking people, organizations, and governments that stood in their way all over the world. He had an idea about how to meet current and future terrorist threats head-on, and when he got back to Washington, he would share his thoughts with President Liu. If the leader of China concurred, neither country would any longer be a punching bag for those who wanted to destroy their way of life.

Completely exhausted, the president finally opened his cabin door and told the agents outside that he was going to sleep. For the next twelve hours, he was true to his word.

As President Ballinger was boarding Air Force One, President Liu's helicopter set down on the lawn of the presidential residence. Later that day, dressed in a tailored blue pinstripe suit with a soft blue shirt and red striped tie, he addressed the nation. In his speech, he emphasized that the rescue had been a joint Chinese-American effort. He thanked both China's Quick Reaction Force and the American Secret Service for their assistance. He also noted, sadly, that Second Vice Premier Ren Shi and industrialist Wang Lei, both of whom had insisted on being present and had provided valuable on-site assistance, had been killed when their helicopter was struck by a ground-to-air missile.

Wearing a hood over his head, Ren Shi was dragged off the helicopter and handed over to the commandant of the Black Prison. To the guards, he was just another nameless prisoner who would be interrogated for information that some nameless bureaucrat deemed important—and then disposed of. This was, however, the first time they'd seen General Chien An accompany a prisoner into the building, which suggested that the person beneath the hood had been important, notorious, or both.

As the commandant and two guards waited outside in the corridor, Chien An escorted the former second vice premier of

China into a holding cell and closed the rusted steel door behind him. Then the general pulled the hood off the prisoner but left his gag and plastic handcuffs in place. Ren Shi was sweating profusely and breathing heavily through his nose.

Withdrawing his 9-mm handgun from his pocket, the general said, "I believe there's only one cure for the disease of betraying one's country, and that's to eradicate the host so it won't infect others." With that, he extended his arm and put two bullets into Ren Shi's head. He then bent down, placed the hood back over the prisoner's face, and opened the door.

"How do you dispose of bodies?" Chien An asked the commandant.

"We throw them in a crematory and then grind the bones to powder."

"Do that immediately. I want to observe the process," ordered the general.

Three and a half hours later, Chien An carried an unsealed plastic bag of grayish powder to his helicopter and placed it on the floor beside him. He instructed the pilot to fly just outside the walls of the prison, to where its sewage treatment plant was located. As the aircraft hovered over the settling basin, the general tossed the bag into the fetid water below.

CHAPTER

17

Standing outside the cave exit through which he'd just crawled, Awalmir Afridi looked around. Every detail of the landscape that he remembered had been erased and replaced with rubble and craters. Grabbing a boulder just to his right, he pulled himself on top of it and continued to climb. Twenty minutes later he reached a small plateau, from where the desolation extended as far as he could see. The attack had decimated the entire area.

Afridi had been set up, and he was furious about it. Someone—possibly even the Great Satan or the Chinese, now that he thought about it—had orchestrated the kidnappings and beheadings so that they could blame it all on him and his followers. He didn't believe the bombings were isolated to this region, and if all of his compounds had been targeted, he'd lost everything.

Afridi turned west toward the Holy Mosque in the city of Mecca. Kneeling, he placed his head to the ground in submission to God Almighty and began to pray. "Glory be to my Lord, the Most High," he began, and then sat up. "All service is for Allah, and all acts of worship and good deeds are for Him. Peace and the mercy and blessing of Allah be upon you, O Prophet." When he reached the end of the prayer, he repeated the cycle a second time.

After the third cycle, Afridi stood up. As he again looked at the desolation before him, a thought occurred. Allah had just spoken to him and showed him how to get his revenge against the infidels.

By the time he returned to the cave opening, it had been widened and his followers were all outside, most of them trying to get the grit out of their hair and clothes. He had expected them to be happy that Allah had spared their lives, so he was surprised at the looks of hostility on their faces. "You let this happen," they told him. Obviously Afridi had lost their admiration.

Angry at their ingratitude, especially after he'd provided them safe shelter in his family cave, he brushed past them and went back into the cave. Looking through the boxes of clothing that were part of the supplies that he'd earlier sent to the cave, he put on a parka, scarf, and stocking cap. From another area he took two blankets, ammunition, food, and several canteens of water and stuffed them into a large backpack. Slinging the backpack over his shoulder and grabbing an AK-47 rifle that was lying against the wall, he left the cave. No one said a word to him, and several of his former followers spit at him as he passed, but Afridi didn't care. They were no longer the nexus of his life. Now he was solely focused on revenge.

On a cold and overcast afternoon, four months after he had last set foot on US soil, Moretti looked out the window of an Air Force C-32, a luxuriously appointed Boeing 757 that was reserved for VIP travel, as it approached Joint Base Andrews. Han Li was on board with him. His recovery was considered a miracle by his medical team, who more than once had believed that they'd be sending his remains to the United States. But the ex–Army Ranger stubbornly refused to die and his recovery had been rapid, thanks to President Liu assigning the best doctors in China to care for him.

During the slightly more than fourteen-hour flight from Beijing International Airport, Moretti and Han Li spent half their time in separate staterooms, each of which contained a comfortable bed and a bathroom with a walk-in shower. They were served two meals and a snack, all prepared by President

Liu's personal chef. Even Moretti, a meat-and-potatoes kind of guy, found the gourmet food exceptionally good. However, after spending four months in a Chinese hospital and eating only local cuisine, he would have traded it in a heartbeat for a cheeseburger and fries.

When they weren't eating or sleeping, he and Han Li talked. Neither considered themselves conversationalists, but the bond between them had grown significantly in recent months. They spoke about their lives, core beliefs, and future ambitions. As a result, the flight passed in the blink of an eye. They were still conversing when the wheels of the 155-foot long aircraft touched down and taxied to a spot not far from the control tower.

Once the engines were shut down, a ramp was pushed to the forward hatch and Moretti and Han Li disembarked. Although the ex–Army Ranger hadn't recovered 100 percent from his surgeries, his physical therapy had gone so well that he was walking ramrod straight and pain-free, something he hadn't experienced in years. When they got to the bottom of the ramp, a Marine Corps major came to attention and saluted, then escorted them to a Sikorsky VH-60N White Hawk helicopter for the ride to Camp David.

The flight to the two-hundred-acre retreat, in the wooded hills of the Catoctin Mountains in western Maryland, took thirty-seven minutes. The pilot touched the six-ton craft down with a barely discernible landing, not far from the presidential cabin. When the White Hawk's rotors stopped turning, the copilot opened the passenger door and unfolded the steps. As Moretti and Han Li stepped into the cold mountain air, they saw a familiar face walking toward them.

"It's good to see you both again," said Bonaquist as he shook their hands. "My life's been boring without you around."

"I thought the Secret Service liked boring," Moretti replied.

"We do. That's just my way of saying that I'm glad to see you. Is that your only luggage?" he asked, pointing to the shoulder bags Moretti and Han Li carried. When they confirmed that it was, he directed the Secret Service agent who accompanied him to place the bags in the cargo compartment of the black Suburban.

"By the way," Moretti said, as they drove to the presidential residence, "I never got a chance to thank you for saving my life. Han Li told me that I'd be dead if you hadn't played doctor."

"You're welcome. But if it's all right with you, I'd prefer that you not tell anyone we played doctor … if you know what I mean."

Moretti and Bonaquist had a good laugh at that. Judging by the look on her face, though, Han Li didn't get the joke.

The Suburban pulled in front of Aspen Lodge, Camp David's presidential residence, a single-story wooden structure containing three bedrooms, two bathrooms, a living room, a dining room, a kitchen, and five fireplaces. The lodge sat in the center of a three-acre clearing at the top of a hill and presented a commanding view of the area.

Bonaquist led Moretti and Han Li through the front door and into the wood-paneled living room, where they saw a group of familiar faces. Seated next to one another on a long, tufted, brown leather couch were Yan He and Doug Cray, along with Peter Cancelliere of the Sixty-Sixty Military Intelligence Brigade in Wiesbaden, Germany, the unit where Moretti was employed as a civilian contractor.

In a matching club chair to their left was President Ballinger. Everyone stood as the president of the United States came forward and, dispensing with decorum, gave Moretti and Han Li each a warm hug. Then he directed them to the mocha-brown fireside chairs to his left while Bonaquist took the vacant club chair to the right of the couch. As the president took his seat, everyone else followed suit.

"How are you feeling?" the president asked Moretti.

"Better than new, sir. While I was recovering from my wounds, President Liu brought in a very talented Chinese surgeon to relieve the back pain that I'd been experiencing for years. The doctor told me that this surgical technique didn't exist a year ago."

"So I've been told," said President Ballinger, "but are you well enough to start working again?"

"I am, Mr. President," confirmed Moretti.

"I'm glad to hear that," said the president, "because we have a lot to discuss in that regard. You and Han Li will be spending the night here. Everyone else is already lodged in either the Dogwood or Birch cabins, a short walk away."

As the president spoke, Moretti glanced at Doug Cray, noticing for the first time the silver oak leaves of a lieutenant colonel on his shoulders. He wanted to congratulate his friend on the promotion, but he wasn't about to interrupt the leader of the free world.

"It's been four months since President Liu and I came within a breath of being executed," said Ballinger. "The intelligence and military organizations of our two countries have produced a multitude of reports analyzing what occurred. However, in our opinion, these thousands of pages of rhetoric are nothing more than bureaucratic storytelling and cover-your-ass documentation. Let me say this in the strongest words possible: Two heads of state are alive today only because of your decisive, out-of-the-box thinking and circumvention of imbedded Washingtonian and Beijing bureaucracy. This allowed you to act quickly and decisively without any interference from pencil pushers." With that, he gestured suggestively at the group before him.

"President Liu and I agree that decision making within the United States and Chinese governments has become arthritic," continued Ballinger. "Diplomatic concerns, protecting one's turf, electoral considerations, and all the other maladies of politics have resulted in bureaucratic inflexibility and made the possibility of taking immediate action against an enemy a rarity. That's why we have decided to create a small, off-the-books organization, answerable only to us, to aggressively act against those who would do our nations harm. Questions so far?"

Moretti nodded to indicate that he had a question, and the

president pointed in his direction. "Why the need for a joint organization?" Moretti asked, wondering if this question would get him an expedited helicopter ride back to Andrews.

"Because China and the United States are joined at the hip to a greater extent than most people realize. We're the two largest economies in the world, together generating as much in global output as the rest of the planet combined. Therefore, what affects either of us invariably cascades to affect every other nation in the world." The president paused to ask if there were any more questions.

Hearing none, he continued. "Now I think it's time to meet the person whom President Liu and I have appointed as the administrative head of this venture, Lieutenant Colonel Doug Cray."

"As some of you already know, and the rest have probably figured out," Cray began, "we're all charter members of this new organization, which will henceforth be known as Nemesis, named after the Greek goddess for retribution against evil deeds. Our operations center will be at the Raven Rock Mountain Complex, the military's backup for the Pentagon, to which we refer as Site R. A 6.5-mile underground tunnel connects Site R to Camp David, which you can use whenever you're here. You can also get to Site R by taking Highway 16, Waynesboro Pike, to Harbaugh Valley Road. However, the best access is to take the 97.5-mile tunnel running beneath the National Security Agency in Fort Meade and the Pentagon. Our offices will be in an isolated area of the complex, where our coming and going won't be obvious. If anyone asks what we do, our cover story is that we perform statistical analysis directly for the office of the president. Hence, it will take the president's permission for anyone outside of this group to enter our offices or, if they're suspicious, delve further into what we do."

"Is this our entire team?" Han Li asked.

"No," said Cray. "General Chien An, chief of the general staff of the People's Liberation Army, and Gao Hui, a member of the Politburo Standing Committee, are also members, but they couldn't be here today. Altogether, Nemesis has eight operational members, plus a limited number of support staff."

Moretti had met General Chien An when he was recovering in the hospital. He liked the stocky general, who he knew would be a valuable member of the team.

Cray continued, "Tomorrow we'll visit Site R, and I'll go into detail about our resources. Until then, let's adjourn and see if we can make a dent in the president's liquor cabinet."

As everyone stood and began to mingle, Moretti walked up to Cray. "Congratulations," he said, extending his hand to his longtime friend. "They couldn't have picked a better person."

"I might say the same, since I'm putting you in operational command of this team," responded Cray.

Stunned, Moretti was just about to ask his friend if he'd lost his mind, when Bonaquist approached and told the lieutenant colonel that the president needed to speak with him. After they left, Moretti wanted a moment to collect his thoughts. Seeing a door that led to the back deck, he decided this was a good time to get away. He'd been standing in the cold mountain air for nearly fifteen minutes when Han Li approached.

"Congratulations," she said.

"You heard?"

"Yes, the president told us."

Nervous, Moretti looked around and saw that he and Han Li were alone. He had wanted to say something to her while they were on the plane, but he hadn't been able to gather the courage to do so—until now. Moving closer, he looked her in the eye and gently said, "I've wanted to ask you if ..."

At that moment, the deck door opened and Cancelliere walked toward them. As usual, he was impeccably dressed in a perfectly tailored charcoal-gray suit with a white shirt and crimson tie. Many people considered the tall, handsome US Army major to be the spitting image of Cary Grant.

"I see you two haven't lost your knack for attracting trouble," he said.

"It's good to see you, Peter," replied Moretti. He was disappointed that he didn't have any privacy to tell Han Li what he'd been thinking about for the past four months.

"In all seriousness," said Cancelliere, "you two did a remarkable job in China."

"Thank you. What do you think of Nemesis?" Moretti asked, putting his thoughts about Han Li on hold.

Cancelliere answered, "Getting rid of the red tape, and keeping what we're doing a secret in a city where inside information has the value of hard currency, will be a game changer."

"That's why Congress isn't involved," said Cray, walking into view. "The navy wouldn't have a ship afloat if it had as many leaks as the Senate and House."

"Do you think you can keep these two under control?" Cancelliere asked Cray.

"Are you kidding?" said Cray, "I can't wait to turn them loose."

"You'll be getting that chance much sooner than you think," President Ballinger said, joining the group. Yan He and Bonaquist followed him onto the deck. Behind them was a navy steward carrying a tray with seven crystal flutes filled with champagne. The president took a glass, and the others followed suit.

"I have an important announcement to make. But before I do, a toast," the president said, raising his flute. "To the bravery, dedication, and daily sacrifice of those in our military, our intelligence agencies, and on this team." Everyone took a sip—except Moretti, who was now a nondrinker.

As the president set his glass back on the tray, his face took on a somber expression. "Now for that announcement. I'd hoped to give you at least a month to get organized before sending you into the field. However, that plan changed a few minutes ago. President Liu and I have been in communication throughout the day. He has what he believes to be reliable information that two nuclear bombs have been smuggled into China. We must assume that whoever is behind this intends to detonate these weapons."

Taking a deep breath, President Ballinger continued, "Consequently, your first mission is to find and capture—or destroy—these bombs without anyone knowing of their existence. Lieutenant Colonel Cray will take you to Site R for a more detailed briefing. After that, you'll be flown to Joint Base Andrews. From there, F-16 fighters will take you to northern China, where the two nuclear devices are believed to have entered the country. I don't have to tell you that if the terrorists find out that we're on to them, they may prematurely detonate these devices. In a country of one and a half billion people, the loss of life and economic fallout would be catastrophic. This is why Nemesis was created. As of this moment you're the predator, and the terrorists and those helping them are the prey. Good hunting."

AUTHOR'S NOTES

The inspiration for the story line of *The Abductions* came to me while visiting the Forbidden City, which was built between 1406 and 1420. Walking through the vast complex, I had to wonder if there were hidden tunnels—and if such tunnels were accidentally discovered, how someone could use that knowledge to their advantage. What followed was an outpouring of this author's imagination.

The historical facts about the Forbidden City are as written in this novel. Located in the center of Beijing, it was home to twenty-four emperors of the Ming (1368–1644) and Qing (1644–1911) dynasties. Encompassing 178 acres, it consists of 90 palaces and courtyards, 980 buildings, and 8,704 rooms, all of which is surrounded by 33-foot-high walls and a 171-foot-wide-by-20-foot-deep moat. It was called the Forbidden City because it was off-limits to ordinary people.

The Palace of Heavenly Purity and the Palace of Earthly Tranquility, where the novel has President Liu and President Ballinger staying, do exist. They were, during the Ming dynasty, respectively, the official residences of the emperor and empress. Connecting these two palaces is the Hall of Union.

The Hall of Mental Cultivation, where Moretti and Han Li spend the night, was both the residence and the office of eight Chinese emperors from the Qing dynasty. The building is divided into a front hall, where the emperor had his throne and conducted business, and a rear hall that served as his bedroom. However, the throne does not rest against the wall. Instead, behind this ornately carved symbol of power is a series of shelves containing books that instruct a new emperor on how to rule over his empire.

There are numerous thrones within the Forbidden City; each is much more ornate than as described in the novel. Creating a chair-like design for the story line made it reasonable that presidential security, suspecting nothing beneath the throne, wouldn't place its ground-penetrating radar above the throne during its security search.

None of the palaces or buildings within the Forbidden City have tunnels beneath them, at least as far as anyone knows. Nor does the Chinese government provide accommodations there for overnight visitors. However, the Grand Hyatt Beijing, the Raffles Beijing Hotel, and the St. Regis Beijing are not far away. All have exceptional overnight accommodations, and nearly everyone working there speaks English.

When you visit the Forbidden City, you should take the pedestrian tunnel under Tiananmen Square to both the Great Hall of the People, which is China's equivalent of Congress, and the National Centre for the Performing Arts. The opera house, part of the NCPA complex, is a magnificent ellipsoid dome of glass and titanium. You enter the building by walking through a hallway that goes underneath a lake that surrounds the structure. It's spectacular.

There is no residential area on the hill across the street from the north gate of the Forbidden City. Instead, that's the site of Jingshan Park, which has a beautiful garden at its base and a flower-lined path running to the top. At the crest, you'll find a pavilion that provides a 360-degree view of the city.

China's domestic surveillance program is massive and continues to grow. The 400,000 cameras cited as being used in Beijing is considered a good approximation by many security professionals.

A trade publication, *China Public Security*, indicates that the Chinese government has spent approximately $16 billion installing cameras nationwide. *China Daily* reports that the city of Wuhan alone has 250,000 cameras. Indeed, most of the country's urban intersections and public squares are under surveillance. Take it for granted that if you're in a Chinese city, you're on camera.

Beijing's population is estimated at 22 million, and Beijing is only seventy-three miles northwest of Tianjin, a city of 15.5 million people. I've driven the Jingjintang Expressway between the two cities many times, though always with someone else at the wheel. Even having served in the military, I don't have enough guts to drive in China. Some liberties were taken in describing the road between these two cities, which is four lanes—not two, and a journey of about an hour. Alas, the mountain pass, reservoir, and utility maintenance buildings don't exist. These were added for the sake of the story line, to place the vans in an unobtrusive hiding place.

Air Force One is the air traffic control sign of any Air Force aircraft carrying the president of the United States. Currently, the president uses a Boeing 747-200B, referred to in military parlance as a VC-25A aircraft. It's based at Joint Base Andrews, which is a short helicopter ride from the White House on Marine One. Boeing is currently working on the next-generation Air Force One, a modified 747-8 aircraft with 4,786 square feet of interior space, nearly 20 percent larger than its predecessor. Its expected delivery date is 2023.

The UH-60 Black Hawk helicopters in Awalmir Afridi's nightmare were based on the Stealth Black Hawks used in the Osama bin Laden raid. In addition, the description of the gear worn by SEAL Team Six is accurate and was taken from *No Easy Day* by Mark Owen. Terrified that he'll end up like bin Laden, Afridi fears that the same helicopters and Special Forces team will come in the middle of the night to his dwelling. That thought should give any terrorist a nightmare.

The Protectors of Islam is a fictional Islamic extremist group headquartered in North Waziristan, a mountainous region of northwest Pakistan near the Afghan border. This lawless area has long been a haven for terror groups, such as the Pakistani Taliban and the Haqqani network, that operate and train here. Razmak, one of three subdivisions of North Waziristan, has a worldwide reputation as a terrorist refuge and is avoided by all who are not in that profession. The United States has, for some time, conducted drone strikes throughout the region.

The defense spending numbers cited by Wang Li to President Liu are accurate. According to an article by Kimberly Amadeo in the February 15, 2018, edition of *the balance*, the US Department of Defense has a 2018 base and overseas contingency operations budget of $700 billion. China's defense budget in contrast, cited at their most recent annual meeting of parliament, is $175 billion.

Abu Sayyaf, which in Arabic means "bearer of the sword," is a Philippine terrorist group based in the southern portion of that country. Initially funded by a Saudi businessman who lived in the Philippines, Abu Sayyaf is believed to have ties to al-Qaeda. They've been involved in kidnappings and beheadings, but they haven't been known to perpetrate these atrocities outside of the Philippines. This group is currently believed to consist of fewer than five hundred members.

Sovereign Industries is a fictional company. Any similarity between it and Norinco, or China North Industries Corporation, which manufactures precision strike systems, anti-aircraft and anti-missile weapons, fuel air bombs, small arms, and a host of other weaponry, is unintentional and coincidental.

The Politburo Standing Committee is the most powerful decision-making body in China. It has seven members, one of whom is the president, and whatever it decrees is de facto the law.

Apologies to the St. Regis Beijing for the fictional carnage and mayhem inflicted on its premises. Lodging there has always been a pleasure, and the staff is extremely gracious and attentive.

It's near the American Embassy, as well as many foreign embassies, which makes the entire area very secure. It's mentioned in this novel that Sovereign Industries is in a fifty-story building just up the street from the hotel, but there's actually no such office tower. And the Starbucks is across the street—not inside the hotel.

China is enormously reliant on foreign natural resources. Without the oil, iron ore, manganese, cobalt, copper, and numerous other minerals necessary to sustain its increasing thirst for energy, the country couldn't maintain its meteoric growth. As it happens, many African countries are rich in the natural resources that China requires. This has resulted in China lending billions of dollars to those countries, enabling them to build the infrastructure necessary to mine and transport their resources for export. According to the *Economist*, China is Africa's biggest trading partner, exchanging $160 billion worth of goods per year. In addition, one million Chinese laborers and traders have moved to Africa in the past decade to support their country's national interests. As a result, the Chinese government has significant clout throughout the African continent. It's therefore not implausible for China to obtain the use of air bases and other military facilities within these countries, as occurs in this novel.

The descriptions of the Navy's Tomahawk, the Air Force's AGM-86C and -86D missiles, and the submarine and aircraft that launched them are all accurate.

It's easy to confuse Inner Mongolia and Mongolia. Inner Mongolia is an autonomous region of China, bordering it to the north and comprising 12 percent of China's total landmass. Mongolia is a sovereign state in East Asia, bordering Russia to the north and China to the south. There's no border crossing between China and Inner Mongolia, since it's all one country. Inserting a fictional border, however, seemed a sensible way to get Moretti and Han Li off-road and introduce the ruggedness of the terrain and the wind turbines.

Since I've driven into Inner Mongolia on several occasions and witnessed the vast numbers of wind turbines and mines spread throughout, it seemed realistic to me to insert both into the story line. If you'd like to see how truly massive a wind turbine is, go to https://www.youtube.com/watch?v=NG1uGt6qUfM, which will give you a new perspective. The basic description of the Vestas V90 is accurate, except for some liberties taken in describing the interior.

The Z-8, Z-10, and Z-9B helicopters are accurately described. However, some liberty was taken with the interior of the Z-8 by placing on board an emergency medical supply locker that contained everything except an operating room.

The Air Force C-32 is the military VIP version of a Boeing 757. I've never been invited to fly in one, so my description of its interior is a marriage of publicly available information and my knowledge of the interiors of other government VIP aircraft. The VH-60N White Hawk is used for transport to Camp David and has a landing pad not far from Aspen Lodge. The presidential residence sits on a three-acre clearing on the top of a hill, and my description of its interior design was obtained from publicly available information.

The description of the Raven Rock Mountain Complex, also referred to as Site R, is factually accurate. Raven Rock is an underground nuclear bunker with thirty-eight communications systems, and it also serves as the alternate Pentagon. A tunnel is said to connect Raven Rock to the Pentagon, via the National Security Agency in Fort Meade—a distance of 97.5 miles. A tunnel is also said to connect Site R and Camp David.

Nemesis doesn't exist, but I've spoken to many people who wish it did. You'll learn much more about this organization in *The Payback*, the next Moretti and Han Li thriller.

Last, this is a work of fiction. As such, the people and companies mentioned within are not meant to depict anyone in the real world.

ACKNOWLEDGMENTS

I am thankful to, and humbled by, an extraordinary group of friends who continue to unselfishly contribute their time and extensive knowledge.

To Kerry Refkin for your constant support, edits, and "outside the box" thinking in providing story line input. You *are* amazing.

To the group—Scott Cray, Todd DeMatteo, John and Cindy Cancelliere, Aprille and Dr. Charles Pappas, Doug Ballinger, Dr. Meir Daller, Alexandra Parra, Nancy Molloy, Mark Iwinski, Mike Calbot, Blair McInnes, Ed Houck, Cheryl Rinell, and David Dodge—for continuing to be my sounding boards.

To Zhang Jingjie for your exemplary research in finding that needle in the haystack.

To Dr. Kevin Hunter and Rob Durst for your feedback on the various technical aspects of computers and cybersecurity.

To Clay Parker, Jim Bonaquist, John Thomas Cardillo, Steve Zhu, and Greg Urbancic for the extraordinary legal advice you continue to provide.

To Corey Fischer, John Lucas, Bill Wiltshire, and Debbie Layport for your superb financial and accounting skills.

To our friends at Jane's Garden Café in Naples, Florida—Zoran

Avramoski, Piotr Cretu, Aleksandar Toporovski, and Billy DeArmond. Thanks for your insights.

To Winnie and Doug Ballinger, and Scott and Betty Cray, thanks for all you've done for the countless people who are unable to help themselves.

ABOUT THE AUTHOR

Alan Refkin is the author of a previous novel, *The Archivist*, and the coauthor of four previously published nonfiction books. He received the iUniverse Editor's Choice Award for *The Wild Wild East* and for *Piercing the Great Wall of Corporate China*. He lectures internationally on how to conduct business in Asia and lives in Florida with his wife, Kerry. He is currently working on his third Matthew Moretti and Han Li novel. More information on the author, including his blogs and newsletters, can be found at alanrefkin.com.

Printed in the United States
By Bookmasters